you can't name an unfinished thing

a novel

by Daphne Kapsali

First published in Great Britain by dk press in May 2015

Copyright © Daphne Kapsali, 2015

The moral right of the author has been asserted.

All rights reserved. No part of this publication may be reproduced, stored in a retrieval system, or transmitted, in any form or by any means, electronic, mechanical, photocopying, recording or otherwise, without the prior permission of the author.

Cover art: Cosmas Xenakis, *Untitled*, oil on canvas, 1960

Printed by CreateSpace

ISBN: 978-1511596244

For Susanne
and Marshall
who did this thing with me.

**you can't name
an unfinished thing**

I have the good seat on the bus, my favourite one in the back, right up against the glass partition, where I can rest my knees and lie back and watch the city go by. These bus journeys are my solace, my reprieve. My time to plug into my music and travel to wherever I want as the bus judders its way through the traffic, south to north and north to south and home again. My time to think, but I didn't think about this. I didn't know I was going to do it.

The phone is in my hand. I type:

'You and I are not done yet. There's a time for us. Not now, but one day.'

The number I haven't used for five years comes up on the screen. I don't remember how it got there. A new phone, a number he's never called me on. I haven't called him for five years. I don't remember putting it in, but I must have done. Typed the number in from memory, saved it. Written his name. Four letters, four taps on the keyboard. His name is on my screen.

I press send.

I kill the screen immediately and stare ahead. I don't want to watch it go. Wash my hands of it, but my fingers are tight around the phone. And the thing I've just done is travelling, unstoppable now, strange scrambled data bouncing off satellites to reconfigure itself into words on another screen. I don't want to imagine it, how he'll lift up his phone and read. I squeeze my eyes shut; my other hand is a fist. I can see it, how he lifts up the phone and reads the words. He doesn't know my number. It's only words, uncredited. He won't reply.

The phone shudders in my hand. My hand is shaking. I swipe and the screen lights up: 'I know.'

'Fuck.' I say it out loud. I slam the phone into my knee, many times, repeatedly, dull thuds. 'Fuck fuck fuck.' A few passengers look over, roll their eyes, mutter to themselves. They do that here: they look. This isn't London. This is as far away from London as I could get.

Not far enough. He knows. The words have reached him, and he knows. And just like that, I'm back exactly where I started, in the palm of his hand like the words I just sent.

We've always liked to play with words. But betrayal is not a word you play with. Betrayal, even if you tell yourself there are reasons. Good reasons, and survival is the best. Survival means killing anything that stands in your way. Except this thing also survives: it wasn't killed. It isn't dead. He knows, and I'm back where I never left.

Betrayal. Not now. A long time ago. And, also, every day.

One

Anna stood in the new room and looked at the boxes and bags at her feet. More bags than boxes, black bin bags and even a few from Tesco, stuffed full of her belongings, some spilling out. There hadn't been time to prepare. She hadn't wanted any more time. She'd taken this flat on the basis that it was available immediately. She'd seen it one day and moved in the next: today. Laura had driven round early in the morning, and they'd put everything in the boxes and the bags. She was the one who'd brought the boxes, otherwise it would have only been bags. Not that it mattered: Anna would have happily left half her things behind, if it meant getting out sooner. She just had to get out.

She stood in the new room and wished she hadn't sent Laura away. Wished she'd accepted her offer to stay and help her unpack. They could have done this together, taken her things out of the bags and found places for them, and made this room look like home. They could have draped something or other over the battered brownish sofa that was now her own, and curled up on it and had a glass of wine. They could have done, but she had sent Laura away, driven by some instinct that she didn't understand. Perhaps it was something to do with bandages and ripping them off, although this was a very weak metaphor for what she knew was coming. She could call Laura and ask her to come back; she could still catch her on her way home. But it would only be postponing the inevitable: there would come a time when she would have to stand in the new room, alone.

She looked down at the boxes and the bags, and got started. She worked for hours, until dim light turned to twilight turned to dark. She broke down the boxes and scrunched up the bags and put them away, and it was finished, and everything was in place. Her duvet on the rickety brass bed in the bedroom, a book on the table beside. Her clothes in the wooden wardrobe with the rusted hinges, that creaked when you opened it. Her toothbrush on the sink in the tiny bathroom, her toiletries lined up around the tub. Her kitchen things in the kitchen cupboards, a plastic chopping board on the counter by the draining board. Her laptop on the desk, along with her lamp and some papers and pens, the rest of her papers in a box underneath. Her books on the shelves behind the sofa, a stack of CDs, three photos in frames. A pink throw with golden borders over the sofa, cushions of many colours scattered around. A rainbow striped rug on the floor in front. The coffee table topped with an ashtray and two purple altar candles, lit. She had lit them, as a finishing touch.

She hadn't cried yet. There had been no time. There had been some words, and a door pulled shut, and nothing, and a night that had somehow passed. There had been a copy of the Loot with a few adverts circled in black ink. There had been some phonecalls, and a pleasant man called Stuart, some papers and a set of keys. There had been Laura and her car and bags and boxes. There was this place, now, this new room full of old things, and Anna standing there, in bare feet on the scuffed wooden floorboards, alone.

Something was terribly, irreparably wrong. It looked like home, but it felt like a set, and all her things, her familiar things, were props. Replicas, because her things were at home, where she lived. It looked liked she lived here, but Anna knew that could not be the case. She lived at home, where her things were, with Jack. And Jack would be coming home soon – it was Tuesday, he went to the pool on Tuesday evenings – and she would probably be in the kitchen. A separate kitchen, a room in itself, not like here, where it shared a space with the living room, appended at the back like an afterthought. Anna would be in the kitchen and Jack would walk in, smelling faintly of chlorine, and he would put his arms around her, and they would stand like that, like always, for a while.

Anna stood in the new room as her life went on without her and now, finally, there was time to cry. Now, there was only time.

*

It's been three weeks, and I've managed to get Sylvia out of her house. We're having coffee on Upper Street, outdoors, pressed close against the window on one of two small tables either side of the door. I don't know what place this is. It's a café, and it has tables outdoors where we can smoke. This is as much as I can take in.

Sylvia is a hostess; she likes all her social interactions at home. She likes giving and welcoming but more than that, I think, she likes the control. It wasn't easy to convince her to come out, but I couldn't face her house. Not the cold, not the memories. I could barely face Sylvia herself, but I needed her. I needed the link, that thin, tenuous thread back into my labyrinth. I needed to see her. I didn't want to talk about it.

She insists on talking. She keeps bringing him up,
'Have you seen him?' she says.
'No.'
'Have you spoken?'
'No.'
She tells me we're being stupid and I cry and she puts her hands on me but she doesn't stop. She doesn't let it go.
'Sylvia, please,' I say. 'I can't do this.'
I don't know if she's my friend. But she's a thread, and I hold on.

She used to tell me, jokingly, that it was a dark tunnel we were in and there was no light. That's how she described her relationship with Chris, her forever relationship that stretched back endlessly into the past, back to long before I met them. A dark tunnel, no light, and she thought I was in there with her, but ours wasn't like that. It was all light and open spaces and I had no desire to be anywhere else. We would look at each other, Jack and I, and smile.

'One day I'll crawl out, on my hands and knees,' Sylvia would continue. 'And then I'll be free.' She'd glance at Chris over her shoulder, challenging him to react. Chris would shrug, relight the end of his spliff and lie back on the floor.

'One day we'll be free, sister! Am I right?' She'd nudge me and laugh.

'Yes, Sylvia,' I'd say, indulging her. 'That's right.'

But later I'd seek Jack out alone, and press myself against him, and tell him I was free but didn't want to be free, not free of him; whatever that meant, I didn't want it.

'I know,' he'd say, and rest his cheek against mine.

She's telling me now that I need to come round on Sunday. I've missed three Sundays already, and it's not the same without me. They'll do a barbeque, she tells me, and it's October. It might be the last.

'Jack will be there,' she says, as if that's a reason for rather than against.

'I can't,' I tell her. 'I can't see him.'

She throws her head back, stares up at the awning, white and navy stripes. She lowers her gaze back down to look at me, lower than it needs to be, like a wolf. 'I don't understand you,' she says slowly. 'I don't understand what happened.'

I start to cry again, and she softens a little. She lights one of her cigarettes and passes it to me. 'You miss him,' she says.

I nod and sob and choke on cigarette smoke.

'Then come.'

I shake my head desperately, no, but she's wearing me down.

'He misses you too. This is stupid.'

And stupidly, I agree.

It's Chris who opens the door. I linger on the doorstep. He gives me a small smile and an awkward hug. I stiffen in his arms, staring at the dark hallway behind him.

'He's not here yet,' he says and gently eases me in. 'Sylvia's just getting ready upstairs.'

In the front room, I drape my coat over the arm of the sofa, though I'll need to put it on again before long. It's always freezing in this house: Sylvia and Chris refuse to

put the heating on. I don't know if it's about economy or preference, but the effect is the same. Jack and I used to come equipped with scarves and extra layers, and sit close together to keep warm. When we got home on Sunday evenings, we'd whack our heating on full blast, remedially, until the room was hot enough to walk around in our underwear. Jack and I like the heat. Our home was always warm.
    'How are you?' asks Chris.
    'All right,' I try. 'Oh, fuck it – you know.'
    He nods. 'Beer?'
    'Sure. Are we having a barbeque?'
    'I thought we might. It's not raining.' We both look outside the windows: not raining, but grey.
    'Let's go outside,' I say. I feel trapped in here. Cornered. Too close to the front door, to the bay windows looking out onto the street. We grab our coats and two beers from the kitchen and go out into the garden in the back.

Chris pokes at the barbeque and I sit on the ledge and smoke and drink my beer and watch him. I sit with my back to the kitchen door, feigning detachment, but every nerve in my body is tuned in to pick up the signals of his arrival, plugged into a psychic alarm system with trip wires all the way from here to the front door. A noise triggers it, and I spring up and spill my beer on my shoes, but it's only Sylvia, bustling out of the kitchen with a plate of halved lemons and a glass of white wine. She comes over and gives me a hug, passing the lemons to Chris behind my back.
    'I'm glad you came,' she says. 'Do you want another beer?'
    I say yes and she goes off to get it, leaving her wine glass balanced on the ledge, next to my empty bottle.
    I turn back to Chris and join him in blowing on the coals to get them to glow red, and the alarm goes off again. I feel it with my whole body. I grab hold of Chris instinctively, his forearm, and he turns sharply, startled, and shoots me a questioning look. But then he hears the kitchen door slam and the scrape of feet on the gravel, and

he understands. He blinks at me, slowly, and gives my shoulder a squeeze with his free hand. And then, as my fingers release their grip on his arm, he turns us both around.

'J-man!' he says, and I manage to raise my hand, like a child in school responding to the roll call. *I'm here.* Jack smiles and his bouncing progress up the garden path is uninterrupted, but he falters; I can see it. He didn't know.

He comes over and he and Chris slap each other on the back and say things that men say in greeting, but he keeps his eyes on me the whole time.

'Hello,' he mouths. I nod and slip past them and walk away.

In the kitchen, I take another beer from the fridge and down half of it before I confront Sylvia.

'He didn't know, did he? You didn't tell him.' I am furious. It's the only thing that keeps me standing up.

Sylvia shakes her head. She doesn't deny it.

'We broke up, Sylvia. It's over. You can't do this.'

'OK. I'm sorry. But I just thought if you saw each other...'

'What? What did you think?'

'Nothing. I just don't understand.'

'No,' I say. 'You don't understand.' I don't understand either, but I can't tell her that. Not when I'm the one who did this thing.

I convince myself to go back out. My legs are cold lead but they convey me to the end of the garden, where both men are bent over the barbeque, watching tears of fat ooze out of the burgers and sizzle as they drip onto the coals. I stand behind them and sip my beer, and Jack twists around and takes a step forward, a step too close. I can smell him; I can feel the heat of his skin. He is tall. Not too tall, but tall enough for his lips to align perfectly with my forehead. But he doesn't rest them there now, like always. He uses them to form words that I don't hear. I look at him, properly. His dreadlocks have been cut short, hedgehog spiky. My stomach flips. His lips move.

'Anna.'
'What?'
'Are you all right?'
'Your hair.'
He reaches up a hand, pats the top of his head. 'Oh yeah,' he says. 'It's all gone! You haven't seen it.'
'No.'
And that's all we say to each other, because I can't be here anymore. I can't be here on another Sunday when nothing is the same, with Jack and his smell and his lips that move but don't touch me and the haircut I knew nothing about, and all the things that will happen and won't happen, all the things I'll miss because of what I did.

'Excuse me,' I mutter and step backwards, away from him, retreat, and then I turn around and I'm practically running, into the kitchen, through the house, out of the door and onto the street and down the street. Running away. Again. I hear Sylvia come to the door, hear her calling my name, but I don't stop. I don't look back, I don't slow my pace until I'm on the bus and I'm clutching onto the rail and still holding a bottle of beer, and the bus is hurtling down the High Street, towards home.

I'm free, but I'm not free. I'll never be free. I don't want to be.

Two

Cat was of the opinion that Anna ought to meet another man. Broaden her horizons. She had actually used the phrase "put yourself out there", which, for Anna, conjured up a picture of a carnival float booming through the streets of London and herself standing on top of it in a shiny leotard and with feathers in her hair and her arms thrown open and a frozen smile on her face. On display. She shared this with Cat and she had laughed and told her she was weird.

'But seriously,' she added. 'You need to get out. This isn't natural.'

But it came naturally to her, staying at home, living quietly with her grief, writing stories that made her cry. So far, all of Cat's suggestions of a night out had been rebuffed. She would concede to go for coffee and, once, even lunch; she could spend hours in Cat's flat in Stoke Newington, and Cat often came over to hers. And she'd been seeing a lot of Laura. Gentle, sympathetic Laura who never pushed her, who would drive over at a moment's notice and sit with her and drink endless cups of tea and listen to her talk, and never criticise. Laura was the only one who'd read her stories, the ones she wrote for herself, surplus to her coursework. They made her cry too, sometimes. Her stories about Jack.

Cat had never cried over a man. Not since school. Anna remembered one evening, when they were seventeen, and she watched her toughest, coolest friend sob after her boyfriend, a year older than them and a Curt Cobain lookalike, had announced the end of their two-week relationship. But it was just the one time, and Cat had not cried since. She preferred to get angry and get on with it, and it was this approach that she advocated with her best friend. Except Anna wasn't angry. She was a lot of things, none of which she had the words for, but she wasn't angry. Cat despaired, and Anna gravitated towards Laura's easy sympathy. And Cat was sympathetic too, and she had gotten her through more than a few days she didn't think she'd survive, more than she cared to remember – but she was also pragmatic. She liked finding solutions more than indulging problems. And she was adamant that the solution to this was going out. Moving on.

Anna could see that it had gone too far. For all her protestations, her *you don't understand*s, for all her friends' patience, she could see that three months of literally crying herself to sleep every night, if she slept at all, was not natural. Cat was right. Still, the idea of going to a bar, at night, on some man-meeting mission made her panic. The idea that there were other men out there made her panic. She had moved out; she didn't want to move on.

'It doesn't have to be like that,' Cat argued. 'We'll go out, we'll have a drink, we'll see what's out there. That's all.'

***

Cat had picked an obscure little bar, some sort of jazz club off the Archway Road. Anna had never been there before, had never even heard of it, for which she was grateful. All places of the past held memories, if not of being there together, then of knowing she'd be going home to Jack at the end of the night. Of the person she'd been when Jack was in her life. Anna couldn't face that person; as with Jack, she'd had to sever all contact to survive.

She wasn't sure about the jazz, however, had never seen the appeal in it, but Cat assured her it wasn't really jazz, not on a Friday night, anyway.

'That's just what they call it,' she explained. 'For effect.'

It wasn't immediately obvious what the intended effect was. The place looked unfinished, somehow, hastily put together. There was a bar as you walked in, and tables and chairs strewn about in no obvious configuration, and a dance floor delineated by a shiny chrome rail, upon which several men were already leaning. And a disco ball dangling from the ceiling.

'It's kind of quaint, don't you think?' said Cat as she led her in by the elbow. They got their drinks, two-for-one cocktails, and found a stretch of rail to lean on. It seemed to be the thing to do.

All too soon, men started circling like vultures. Anna felt herself shrinking, leaning closer to Cat for protection.

'It's OK,' Cat soothed. 'Just talk to them. Or don't.' She lifted her glass to a man who'd just winked at her from across the room, and squeezed Anna's hand.

Guys came over, offered drinks, asked questions, wandered off. Some danced in their vicinity, with hopeful eyes. One held his hand out to Anna as he swayed his hips but she said thank you, no, I don't want to dance, and he moved on. Most approached Cat first – Cat, the most beautiful girl in most places – and she chatted to them easily without encouraging, without giving anything of herself away. She was here for Anna, to give Anna a glimpse of the world that carried on.

'What about him?' she said, tilting her head to indicate a dark-haired, happy-looking man swigging from a bottle of Corona. A good-looking guy, jeans hanging off him in the right way, muscles rippling nicely as he moved, Anna could see. Her reaction was entirely encyclopaedic.

'Yeah, he seems nice.'

'Nice? That man is sexy!' Cat laughed.

'It's not Jack.'

Cat put her drink down and wrapped her arms around Anna's shoulders. 'I know,' she said into her hair. 'It's shit.' She pulled away, slid her hands down to Anna's arms. 'The point is, there are other guys out there. Nice, funny, sexy guys. But they won't be Jack. They will never be Jack.'

It was like a death sentence, her friend's words of encouragement, offered in earnest, in hope. Never. Anna felt sick. She thought her legs would give way but, inexplicably, she was still standing. She stared down at her feet.

'Look, we don't have to do this,' Cat said quickly. 'We can go. Just say the word and we'll go.'

If only she'd said yes, then. If only she'd told the truth, that she wanted nothing more, in that moment, than to leave. If only she'd left, still sober, with her friend, and gone home. But she shook her head and said no, and when the next man came along and asked if she wanted a drink, that's when she said yes. To the wrong question, too late.

She wasn't sure when she'd pressed the self destruct button but she could tell, by the adrenaline rushing through her, making her feel completely reckless, that the countdown had begun. She could tell, too, by the nervous glances that Cat was giving her, the way she kept asking if she was alright.

'I'm fine,' she lied, and there was a strange joy in it, in knowing what she was about to do.

The man – he said his name was Dom – was about her height, and smelled of aftershave and mildew. He had dark, twinkly eyes and bushy eyebrows and a small, pink mouth that he kept pressing into her neck. She let him. She let him put his tongue in her ear, and whisper hoarsely how he wanted to take her home, and the things he would do to her there. She let him put his hands on her arse and grind up against her as his tongue found its way into her mouth. It was around this time that she stopped taking part in the proceedings. She was led out of the bar and onto the street, led by the hand by Dom as Cat protested, was told to stay out of it, and gave up. Into a taxi and to Dom's first floor flat, somewhere in Crouch End. Onto a rumpled bed, after several items were pushed off it. The bed smelled of mildew, too, sheets that hadn't dried properly.

He's probably a decent enough guy, under different circumstances, she thought as her clothes were hastily removed and Dom collapsed on top of her. It was no consolation: it wasn't Jack. It would never be Jack. And the person who had once held Jack in these arms that now lay limply by her sides was suffocating under another man's weight. These arms, this body, betraying who she'd been. Killing her to survive. She noted the complete absence of affection in the way Dom pounded and grunted on top of her, and she slipped out of this body of a stranger and watched it happen. Watched a man fucking a woman, doing to her all the things he'd said he'd do. And she thought: from now on, I'll only exist in the third person. It was safer there, once removed.

But in her stories, in the first person, it would be Jack. It would always be Jack.

*

Toby calls me. He calls me periodically, every few weeks, though we don't see each other that often.

'Have you heard from Boo?' he asks.

'His name is Jack,' I snap, irrationally, though the answer is no. It's been four months. Longer, almost five.

His name is Jack, for Jackson, but they call him Boo. It started off as Blue: his mum's Jamaican but he got his Irish dad's blue eyes. Blue, but he couldn't say it. The story goes he used to pull himself up on bandy toddler legs and pat his chest with his hand and say 'Boo!', introducing himself to the world. And it stuck.

I wouldn't mind Boo if it weren't for the hip-hop culture connotations. To me, Boo is Boo Radley, the mysterious and misunderstood unlikely hero of *To Kill a Mockingbird*. My favourite character, in one of my favourite books. This Boo I could live with, but not the one peddled by people like Usher and Alicia Keyes. He can stay right out of my house.

'I think I read it in school,' Jack said when I told him. 'Would I have read it in school?'

'I don't know. Maybe. I don't know what they teach you in school over here.'

I bought him a copy soon after. He didn't read it. He meant to, he said, but the time was never right. He's more of a non-fiction man, anyway. *How To* manuals and the secrets of famous hackers.

He introduced himself to me as Jack, so that's what I call him. Jack, or J. Or nothing at all. I don't need to call him anything. I know who he is.

'You never talk?' Toby wants to know.

'No,' I say. 'There's nothing to talk about.'

I can tell he wants to ask but, then, again, he doesn't want to get involved.

'Fair enough,' he concedes. 'What are you up to this weekend? You want to get pissed?'

'No Jack.'

'No Jack.'
'Yes, please.'
Toby, Chris and Jack have been friends since their early twenties. I don't know how they met and they've never told me; they're not secretive about it, exactly, but not forthcoming either. All three of them enjoy being somewhat mysterious, although Jack genuinely is. The other two try to emulate him but, as white English boys to his Irish-Jamaican mystique, they never quite pull it off to the same degree. There are references to basketball and card games and "them days down south" and names of people I've never met. I let them wash over me, comment if I'm included, but never ask. Jack tells me the stories of himself that he wants me to know. The rest is background noise, the chatter of friends, their private history.

We meet in the Punch & Judy in Covent Garden. Hardly original, but he lives south and I live north and this is somewhere in between. I find him at the bar downstairs, leaning on his elbows, chatting to the barmaid. There is an empty pint glass in front of him. I scan the vicinity for signs of Jack.
'Relax,' Toby says when he spots me. 'I wasn't gonna trick you. Nobody here but me.'
I slide in next to him, kiss him on the cheek, point to his glass.
'What are you drinking?'
'Carlsberg,' he says, so I order him another and a vodka and cranberry for myself, and we find a table.

Toby is sharply dressed, as usual, in a tailored charcoal grey suit, a black shirt and black pointy, shiny shoes. Coupled with a cheeky grin and easy South London charm, he can pull this look off and carry it anywhere, from the office to the pub and everywhere in between, via private members' clubs and his dealer's place off Coldharbour Lane.
'That jacket looks soft. Is it soft? Can I touch it?' I touch it anyway, without waiting for permission. I put my hand on his shoulder and run it down his arm.

'You're a freak,' Toby says. 'Stop touching me.'
'Is it angel hair?'
'I don't know, mate. Probably. It was fucking steep.'
'But so worth it,' I drawl, mockingly. I'm enjoying myself. I haven't had a night out since the jazz club incident, but being here with Toby, despite my reservations, is painless. He is another thread that I could tug on, but I don't.

We talk about my course, a Masters in Writing that I started in October, and my part-time job at a yoga centre, where the clients greet me with *Namaste*. Toby laughs and calls them pretentious wankers, while I urge him to come and try a class. He tells me anecdotes about his colleagues and a girl he's been seeing, on and off. He asks about Cat. The two of them went out briefly a few years ago; it's how Jack and I met. I fill him in on Cat's news, and he looks wistful for a moment. They're friends now, and it's been a long time, but Cat isn't someone you get over easily. I tease him about this, but gently, and he snaps out of it. And just when I think I'm safe in these shallow waters of uncomplicated pub chat, he brings up Jack and, as always, the breath leaves my body.

'So you haven't seen him at all?'
I shake my head. 'One time, at Chris and Sylvia's.' Toby nods; he's heard about that. Sylvia has reported on my abrupt departure. 'Not since.'
'What happened with you guys anyway?'
'He's your friend. What did he tell you?'
'He told me nothing. You know Boo: he doesn't talk.'
'He talks when he wants to.'
Toby smiles. 'He doesn't want to. He doesn't want to talk about this.'
'About me.'
'About you.'
'Nothing?'
'Not a word. He just changes the subject.'
It's my turn to smile: Jack is excellent at changing the subject. You don't even know he's doing it, half the time.
'Shocking.'

Toby laughs. 'So what happened?'
'I left.'
'I got that, but why?'
I shrug. My hands begin to shake. I rip a beermat to shreds and reach for some words. 'We just. I just. I don't know.' I can't do it. I can feel the tears coming and I can't do this here. 'You know, I don't want to talk about it either.'
Toby throws his arms up in resignation. 'You two were made for each other,' he says without thinking. His eyes widen. 'I'm sorry. Mate, I'm sorry.' He puts his hand on top of mine, presses down.
'Fuck,' I remark.
'Yeah, it is a bit like that. Another drink?'
'Tequila.'
We get drunk.

We stagger outside just past eleven. We hold on to each other for balance. I rub my cheek against his sleeve, like a cat. 'So soft,' I purr. 'Angel hair.' I think it's hilarious.
'Get off me!' Toby laughs. But then he goes serious. I know, because he says my name urgently, 'Anna,' and draws his breath in slowly, deliberately, as if preparing for a speech. 'It's true, what I said before. I'm sorry, but you were.'
'Fuck,' I say again. I don't want to hear this. I want to hear this more than anything. 'I'm fucked. I fucked up.'
Toby straightens himself, attempts to look me in the eyes. 'I'm sure you had your reasons,' he says. 'Come on. It's not that bad.'
But it is. It's true. We were. And it is that bad.

Three

She had her reasons. Good reasons; reasons compelling enough to warrant doing what she did. She must have had.

'We need to see this character's motivation,' her tutor had said, towards the end of a workshop that had almost brought Anna to tears. She had submitted a story – not a Jack story but a story, nonetheless, about Jack – to the group for critique. Each week, they workshopped one piece of writing, and today had been her turn. It hadn't gone well.

They were ruthless, her fellow students. They seemed to think that being harsh equalled being helpful, and that praise should always be tempered by a but. Constructive criticism: that's how they justified it. Constructive, tearing everything apart. But it wasn't their fault. This is what they did with every piece they were given. This is what they were encouraged to do. They had no idea they were talking about her life; that it wasn't her words she was being called upon to defend, but her actions. The choices she'd made, that she couldn't explain.

'I'd say this is a very good first draft,' David had said, kindly, completely unaware of the irony of his comment. 'It's got potential, but you need to develop it further.'

Anna had nearly laughed.

Loosely autobiographical, she'd called it, a short story about the end of a relationship that wasn't hers and Jack's. Except she'd made nothing up. She'd given the characters different names (Moira and Declan: they were Irish) and moved them to Liverpool, but she'd been writing from within the story and she couldn't see her way out. She had become trapped in the first person narrative, Moira's perspective, and her view was constricted by events, actual facts. Write about what you know, that's what the tutors always told them, and this is what she knew. She could imagine a different outcome, but it was fantasy; she had been faithless in life, but in her fiction she was paradoxically faithful to the truth. It was autobiography, wearing a costume: there was nothing loose about it.

'All I see here is some girl who's left her boyfriend for no good reason,' was Janet's contribution, eloquent as always. 'She doesn't get my sympathy.' Janet was the least likeable member of their group and she had not managed a single positive comment about anyone's work so far, almost eight months into the course. She was loud and brash and, at 22 to Anna's 26, arguably a bit too young to be so opinionated. Anna didn't normally mind. She'd been subjected to Janet's caustic tongue before and, like everyone in the group, she had learned not to take it personally. Except this time it was personal and that, again, was Anna's fault. Her mistake. Do not use your writing as therapy: they had been warned about that too.

It is never a *good* reason, Anna thought resentfully, but she knew this was just playing with words. She had been good at it once. She could make words into anything, twist them and turn them and have them do her bidding. Now she couldn't even make a sentence to explain herself. And those people kept asking. They kept asking why.

Why had Moira left Declan? Why had Anna left Jack?

Declan had pulled away from Moira; he grew distant and withdrawn, he shut her out. Moira tried to be patient, understanding, give him space, wait it out. She had faith; she and Declan had never strayed far from each other before. But time went by and nothing changed; Declan refused to talk, and Moira got scared. She started looking for reasons until, one day, she found a girl's phone number on his desk. Infidelity, she thought: that was a reason. When confronted, Declan neither confirmed nor denied it; he remained distant and withdrawn. Moira couldn't handle the possibility, the not knowing. The distance between them, as they lived side by side. Moira chose to make the distance tangible. Moira left.

The distance between them: that was what Anna couldn't live with. The phone number was disconcerting, a crumpled bit of paper, a corner torn off something larger, casually emptied out of Jack's pocket one evening, along with a yellow lighter, a USB stick and a wrapper, golden, from a chocolate or a sweet. "Jayne" it said, and it was written in eyeliner. The phone number had come at the wrong time, and she'd asked the wrong question, trusting in an honesty she had never questioned before.

'Should I be worried?' she'd asked. And Jack had simply said no. When Jack wanted to play with words, there was no one, not even Anna, who could beat him. But before, they had always played on the same team. She didn't know how to play against him, or why.

'I love the characters,' said Stella, the closest thing Anna had to a friend in the group. 'And like David said, it's got potential. But the thing is, to be honest, I think Moira overreacted a little. She could have tried to find out for sure.' She was gentle, perhaps suspecting there was more of Anna in Moira that she'd admit.

She could have tried. But that wasn't the thing. The thing was the thing between them that the unfathomable distance was stretching out, stretching out of shape. It was a thing that was good through and through. In over three years, Anna and Jack had never fought, never raised their voices in anger or lowered them in hurt. It wasn't that they agreed on everything, only that they cared more about being happy than being right. They were natural teammates, and a win for one was a win for both. It was a simple thing, a togetherness, pure and easy, without discussion, without design. She didn't want it frayed, not even at the edges, not tainted by things suspected and things unsaid and things that needed to be said, and couldn't. She could have asked, but she didn't. She didn't want to play against Jack.

'It's just the way it ends, you know? It's not believable. It's not *reasoned* enough,' Tim had added, before their tutor took over to supply the final remarks.

It wasn't, Anna agreed. She couldn't believe it either, but she had written it the way it happened. It wasn't believable, and it was true. But true doesn't always make for a good story. Not one that anyone wants to read. Next time she'd invent fictions for them to pick apart, instead of submitting her life to be judged for literary merit. It was a mistake, using her writing as therapy: this hadn't been therapeutic at all.

As she was gathering up her things to leave, Stella came and stood next to her.

'Are you alright?' she asked.

Anna nodded.

'It's a good story,' Stella said. 'It just needs a bit of rewriting.'

If only, Anna thought, but kept the bitterness out of her smile.

'Thank you,' she said. She took Stella's arm and together they walked out of the building.

***

Anna stopped by the pool on the way home. She still paid her monthly membership to the local gym, the gym that had been her local when she lived with Jack. They had joined together, but went separately, on different days. If he didn't change his routine, Anna could still go for a swim a couple of times a week without too much of a risk of running into him, glistening, doing his butterfly stroke. Anna didn't do that; she could manage a basic breaststroke at best. She wasn't a strong swimmer, but she liked being in the water. This, along with yoga, was the only form of exercise she could tolerate. She stuck to the off-peak hours and shared the pool mostly with pensioners on doctor's orders, whose slow, haphazard progress up and down the lanes matched her own. Peak times were for the fast and the serious, and that's when Jack went. Tuesdays and Thursdays after work, sometimes a weekend morning.

It was four pm when she got there, and the pool had a single occupant, and old lady treading water in a floral shower cap at the shallow end. Anna changed into her swimming costume and joined her. She didn't feel like exerting herself. She just wanted to get her head under the water, immerse herself in the soundless blue, put a pause in her day before going out to meet Cat. She didn't feel like doing that either. The workshop had taken it out of her completely, and all she wanted to do was hide in her flat, alone. But she did that far too often, and she had promised. Cat had a new boyfriend, Dylan, and she wanted Anna to meet him.

She did a few reluctant laps, underwater, and finally emerged at the deep end of the pool, hooked her legs over the edge and lay back, floating, with her eyes closed. There was a slight commotion, echoey voices and the splatter of feet on the wet floor. Three white girls, pale as sour milk, late teens or early twenties, boobs spilling out of bikini tops which were, strictly, not allowed. But no one really bothered with the rules at off-peak times. They were loud as they splashed their way into the water, and Anna could imagine her shower-capped friend shaking her head and tutting, though she had her back to the four of them. Anna dipped her head back to drown out the noise. When she lifted it out again, she could hear the girls chatting, dropping names, calling each other "man" a lot. She tuned them out, focused her mind on the gentle splashing of the water around her ears, until she heard his name. Boo. With her heart thumping in her chest, Anna told herself this was the generic Boo, an RnB reference to one of the girls' boyfriends. Not her Boo Radley. Not Jack.

'I seen him here, Tuesday night,' said girl number one.

Fuck. Anna slid her legs back into the water, held on to the side of the pool with her head still turned away from the shallow end, and tried to breathe.

'Man, he is *fit*,' asserted girl number two.

'Innit.' Number three.

'Bit old though.' Number one again.

'Nah, man: mature. Wouldn't kick him out of bed, you know what I'm saying?'
'Yeah man Trish, if he ain't good enough for you, I'll have him.'
'You keep your hands off him, you skank!' This, presumably, from Trish.
Laughter.
'You talk to him then?'
'We chatted, innit.'
'You know I heard he's single.'
'I never seen him with no girl.'
'I'm telling you, man. Mick said, at reception. He had this girl, but they split.'
'You joking with me now.'
'Nah, Trish. Some white girl, Mick said. I axed, didn't I?'
'Silly bitch,' Trish remarked. 'If I had a man like Boo, no way I'd let him go. You hear me?'
Anna did. Anna heard her. She didn't want to hear any more. She hoisted herself up and over the edge of the pool, retrieved her flip flops and her towel and ran, as fast as she could go without slipping, into the changing rooms. Into a toilet cubicle, where she pressed her hands against the door, dry heaving tears that wouldn't come, and watching a small puddle form around her feet.

***

If the point of the evening was for the new boyfriend to impress the best friend and earn her approval, Dylan was clearly not aware of it. If anything, it felt like he was checking Anna out, rather than the other way round. He took her proffered hand and gave it an earnest squeeze, but said nothing. He regarded her through narrowed eyes.
'You don't *look* Greek,' he said suspiciously. 'You're too dark.'
'Oh. Sorry about that.'
'Yeah. You know the ancient Greeks are supposed to have been blond and fair skinned?'

'I've heard that rumour, yes.'

'Cat's one of them,' he said, with obvious satisfaction. They both turned their heads to contemplate the blonde and fair skinned Cat, her long, lean body draped over the bar, in the process of ordering drinks. She caught them looking and winked.

'A Greek goddess,' Anna offered.

'That's what I call her,' Dylan said drily. 'Can you speak Greek?'

'Despite my dark skin? Yes.'

'Can you teach me?'

'Um. I'm not sure I'm qualified.'

'I heard you've got a degree in literature and a Masters in writing,' he challenged.

'Two thirds of a Masters. And my fellow students completely trashed my work today.'

'Yeah? Fuck them. You're a misunderstood genius.'

Anna shuddered. His words were almost an exact echo of Jack's, of the praise he gave her randomly, casually, taking away her doubts before they'd even had a chance to form. There was nothing deliberate about it, no trace of trying to say the right things, no agenda. 'You're the best,' he'd say simply. 'You're a genius.' And Anna was. With Jack, she was the best she could be.

She recovered her composure, looked straight at Dylan.

'You just met me,' she challenged.

'Yeah?'

'I might be a shit writer.'

'True. So show me. Let me read your stuff.'

'I just met you.'

'So you said.'

'OK. Maybe,' Anna said, defeated. She changed the subject. 'Greek's not an easy language to learn, you know.'

'I'm not a complete beginner.'

'Meaning?'

Dylan gave her a mysterious smile, and quoted the first few lines of the Odyssey in perfect ancient Greek. His Cardiff accent wrapped around the Greek words made for a very bizarre experience.

'What the fuck?' Anna said.

Dylan grinned. 'I'm Welsh. We're into dead languages.'

'Did you study literature then?'

'Nope. I'm an electrician. But,' he added, 'I was named after Dylan Thomas.'

Cat returned from the bar and handed out drinks and slipped her arm through Dylan's.

'What are you two talking about?' she asked.

'Homer,' Anna replied. 'And Dylan Thomas.'

Cat groaned. 'For fuck's sake,' she muttered. 'Where do I find you people?' But she looked happy.

Later, when Dylan had been dispatched to the bar for another round of drinks, Cat tugged on Anna's sleeve.

'So?'

'I like him.'

'Me too.' Cat smiled, and then she leaned closer, conspiratorially and unnecessarily, because there was no one around to hear. 'Who's Dylan Thomas?'

Cat was an academic – she was studying for a PhD in Art Theory – but the world of poetry was a foreign land, and Anna was her guide; she gratefully defaulted to her knowledge for all things literary.

'Welsh poet,' Anna supplied.

'Does he look like him?'

'In the hair, maybe. But your Dylan is much better looking.'

Cat broke into a dreamy smile. 'I love those curls. And the eyes. Did you see his eyes?'

'I saw.' They were a sort of dark grey, speckled with blue, and very intense when he turned them on you. They were hard to miss.

'I keep thinking how he'd really get on with Jack. I can just see them together.' Cat stopped talking abruptly, regretting, perhaps, her slip, the mention of his name. Her face contracted with worry.

But Anna saw it, too, the similarities between the two men, the intensity and the openness they had in common. She saw Jack standing there next to her, touching her lightly, a part of his body always in contact with hers, as he fell into his usual teasing banter with Cat, and drew Dylan easily into a new friendship. She saw the four of them together on many more evenings like this, as they would have been, and she wondered, again, about the end of her story.

'I know,' she told Cat. 'I've been thinking the same.' And she could have told her then, about the workshop and the girls at the pool and the reasons she questioned. She could have brought Jack into their evening, fleshed him out with words, felt the ghost touch of his hip against hers, the tips of his fingers beating a tune on the small of her back. She looked at her friend's kind, eager face, suspended between the duty of friendship and the excitement of a new maybe-love, and she knew that Cat would choose the former without question, wouldn't hesitate to push everything else aside to make room for Anna's pain, again. But she shouldn't have to make that choice tonight. Tonight was about curls and eyes and the way Dylan had looked at Cat when she was leaning over the bar.

So that's what she told her, instead. She chose friendship tonight. Her pain, her questions would keep. Jack would keep. Anna kept him. Despite having let him go, she kept him, always, by her side.

*

It's Jack's birthday. 35 years. Nine months.

If this were a story, I would call him and say happy birthday. I would say *I miss you* and he'd say *I know, I miss you too*.

If this were a story that made sense, a well-reasoned story, there wouldn't be a phonecall at all. There would be 35 years, a celebration, and there would be no nine months to subtract. There would be nine months added to our years – unceremonious, unnoticed, taken for granted – and we'd only be counting candles on a cake. Jack wouldn't like it, the candles and the cake, but I'd do it anyway. I'd bake the cake myself, and cover it in icing, and he'd forgive me. Jack always forgives me, and he can always be swayed with something sweet.

32 years. First birthday. 'I don't want presents,' Jack warns. 'I don't want cake, I don't want candles.' So I get him a family size bag of M&Ms and scatter them all over my bed – white sheets for contrast – and spell out 32 in the centre. I hold my lighter up to his face until he gives in and blows the flame out.

'What did you wish for?' I ask and, for all the cheesy lines that his eyes betray, he only smiles.

We feed each other M&Ms and kiss a lot.

33 years. We have a barbeque in the garden, though the day starts off drizzling, and serve our friends pork chops, beef burgers and Portobello mushrooms, with cupcakes and chocolate éclairs for dessert. I experiment with making pina coladas, mainly because we've just acquired a blender and I want to play; most people opt for beer. The sky clears up and an afternoon of intermittent sunshine is followed by a mild June evening, with tealights dotted around the garden, and people lying on throws and blankets on the grass. Toby insists on leading everyone into a drunken

rendition of happy birthday, on purpose, to mess with Jack, and Jack looks suitably uncomfortable and shuffles from foot to foot and holds on to my hand as he smiles his way through it. A few spliffs are passed around and suddenly the éclairs and cupcakes, largely ignored earlier, become very popular. Once all our guests have gone home, we fall into bed, limbs casually tangled up, and share a half-smoked spliff and the last cupcake.

'Was that very traumatic?' I ask. 'The singing?'

'It wasn't too bad,' he says. 'This is better. This is the best.'

34 years. We spread the word that Jack doesn't want to celebrate his birthday this year, and stay at home. We spend £50 on Chinese takeaway and eat it on the living room floor, out of the plastic containers, with our hands when the chopsticks fail us. After dinner, I light a sparkler and wave it around ritualistically as Jack unwraps his fortune cookie, which stands in for cake. He reads: 'Love is as necessary to human beings as food and shelter.' Mine: 'You can make your own happiness.' We ponder these for a while, and count them off on fingers stained dayglo pink from the radioactive sweet and sour sauce: love, food, shelter, happiness. We have it all. We turn off all the lights and draw shapes and words for each other in the dark with the remaining sparklers.

'I want all my birthdays with you,' Jack says.

'Done,' I promise.

35 years. He could be with Trish now, some Trish or other, some pale-as-milk twenty-year-old who thinks he's hot and calls him Boo. He isn't – I know this the same way I know that I have a pulse – but that's no consolation because he could be, because of me, silly bitch. Because I let him go. Because nine months ago, I did the one thing I said I wouldn't. The one thing I never thought I'd do. Nine months ago, I stood behind the door of our home when I heard the scrape of his key on the other side, and as soon as he pushed it open I said 'I'm done. I can't do this anymore.' He

had been halfway through a smile. 'OK,' he said softly, and took one small step back and pulled the door closed again, gently, with barely a click. And I preserved the thing I was protecting, I kept it intact, but I think I broke his heart. And he'll forgive me, and if there is the opposite of consolation, then it is this.

This is a draft. I hold the phone in my hands and I look at it and I bring up his name in the contacts. I don't call. I don't text. Nine months.

Four

Anna spent the summer writing her thesis, the first few chapters of a novel that she described as literary fantasy, which was about a race of people who came in different colours – purple, green, turquoise, fuchsia – that determined their purpose and status in society. Those of a turquoise hue, known as Turqs, were the most highly evolved and regarded, spiritual gurus who reigned over all the other colours. She didn't have a title yet. This creative part was to be accompanied by a critical essay on a relevant topic; in Anna's case, racism as portrayed allegorically in contemporary literature.

She hadn't felt like a holiday. She couldn't face the beaches and the brightness and the possibilities that holidays entailed. Greece was out of the question; the London version of summer suited her better this year. She opened the bay windows on those days when the sun came out, let its warmth and the traffic fumes infuse her living room as she worked, and it was enough. She'd finished the thesis in August and taken a week off in Athens, catching up with friends and family, but she'd spent most of it longing to get back to the quiet of her flat, and the safety of Cat and Laura, who knew how to listen, and Toby and Chris, who knew not to ask. And the girls from work, her yoga buddies, who knew nothing at all.

Her friends in Athens had lost patience much sooner than their London counterparts. They'd said the right things at first, but they'd never met him, never seen her with Jack. It made sense, once you saw them together. Everyone said so who had, but those who hadn't said other things. They said things like "Plenty more fish in the sea" and "Time heals all wounds". They only saw Anna, alone, and a length of time sufficient to have healed. They saw fish, and recited lists of their single friends. They asked too many questions. Like her workshop group in university, they kept picking holes in her story, digging up things that she didn't want dug up. She didn't know what to do with them and the questions that they dragged along, long, gnarly roots that went deeper than she wanted to go. She wasn't being deliberately obscure, but she was tired of giving an explanation that met with blank stares and another round of questions. This wasn't a story she could rewrite so that it made more sense; this wasn't a story that she'd write at all.

The story she did write – her thesis – earned her a Merit; she submitted it in September and received her degree, but she didn't attend the graduation ceremony. She put her Masters, in its frame, in the box under her desk that served as a filing cabinet, and put her novel on hold; somewhere between August and September, a few chapters before the end, she'd lost her momentum. She still enjoyed her job, so she switched her hours to full time and slipped quietly into that world of *Namaste* and daily yoga classes, where she could stand at the reception desk and answer every single question, and no one expected of her anything more than that. At the end of the month, when her lease was up, she moved in with Laura, into a two bedroom flat in Finsbury Park. They kept a bottle of Baileys, always, in a cupboard, and cooked dinner together in the evenings. They watched a lot of DVDs. Anna pushed furniture out of the way and demonstrated yoga poses in the living room to relieve Laura's stress, and Laura tried to get Anna to eat more fruit. A year had passed, thirteen months, and everything was different. And it was the same.

It wasn't her friends' reactions that were the problem. It wasn't their waning patience, their insistence that she should move on. It was the sameness, how she felt, that didn't change. She was learning to live with it, teaching herself tricks and strategies for survival and, on the outside, it was working. On the outside she smiled and made jokes, and she was kind again, and giving, having finally shed the absolute self-centredness of grief. She looked like herself again, and she was. Herself, but without Jack: acutely, incomprehensibly, still. She didn't talk about him, except, rarely, to Cat and Laura, sporadic confessions of missing him that she knew they wouldn't push any further than that. She didn't cry. There were times when she felt happy, unburdened – but never quite free.

Moving on: she tried it. She went on a few dates, looking for Jack in other places when she couldn't find him at home. She looked for him in other men, parts of him in the absence of the whole: a gesture, the shape of his eyes, a pair of shoes. She didn't do it consciously, but these small pieces of familiarity made it possible for her to say yes when these men who weren't Jack asked her out. It made it possible to agree on times and places, get dressed up and go out to meet them, but when she found herself there, with these men, in pubs and bars and, one time, her flat, when one of them insisted on seeing her home, those pieces didn't add up. She would sit there, with a drink in her hand, answering questions about her job and the music she liked and dutifully asking the same, but these weren't dates, they were interviews: casting sessions for a role that was already taken. These men, who didn't know they had been chosen for their similarities to another, and tried to win Anna over with whichever qualities they considered best, were doomed to failure: they were expected to play Jack, but they insisted on being themselves. They might have the hair or the height or the job in IT, but they spoke to her with words that sounded foreign, they looked at her with strangers' eyes, they tried to touch her with hands that weren't Jack's. She never saw any of them more than once, and even cut a few evenings short, making up excuses to go home after the first drink. The persistent man, a better candidate than most, got as far as kissing her on her sofa, but he retreated swiftly when she burst into tears.

'I'm not doing this anymore,' she told Laura that evening. 'It's pointless.'

And Laura, who had encouraged her into every date so far, who'd found something nice to say about every one of those men, who'd gotten her dressed and out the door on each occasion and poured her a glass of Bailey's when she returned, freshly devastated, from another evening that hadn't added up to Jack, and had remained hopeful throughout, nodded, this time, and said nothing to change her mind. This time she nodded as if she agreed.

She wasn't free, and it began to scare her. The thing she had chosen to save when she fled – not herself, not Jack, but the thing between them – had an appetite for living. She'd thought she could stand it up against a wall and execute it, give it a dignified death, a clean and final end as befitted it, but the thing refused to be killed. There was no severing of ties, no matter how much she hacked at them with time and tricks and reason; if anything, they seemed to grow stronger, like the roots of trees, thicker and deeper, more established with each passing season. It all looked different on the outside, but inside, Jack continued to grow. It wasn't even a matter of scratching the surface; it was but a fine coating of dust that kept them apart. You only had to blow on it and the true picture was revealed, right beneath the veneer of her everyday life. Anna tried to avoid conditions that would cause this to happen, but there was always a draft sneaking in from somewhere, blowing the dust into her eyes. Like Tinkerbell's fairy dust, taking her right back to the Neverland where she and Jack still shared a bed.

It wasn't her friends' reactions, it wasn't what other people thought or the mathematical formula that dictated she should be over it by now; what had begun to scare Anna was the cold, creeping suspicion, like a chill up her spine, that the right decision wouldn't feel so wrong. There would be some redemption by now, if leaving had been the right thing to do. She had begun to fear that this was something fated, some sort of destiny, and she had gone against it, and the words she had spoken softly, the gentle closing of the door had actually been a violent act, forever seeking restitution, until she put it right. Was it hubris to wrench apart what destiny had conspired to unite? Could there be atonement for such a thing? Destiny was a lovely word when they had lain together and told each other it was meant to be. Now it was terrifying, an avenging force that wouldn't be denied, and what had begun as a suspicion gradually morphed into understanding, and solidified into words: *this isn't over yet.*

Yet: a threat and a promise. Yet – not Neverland. It was strangely liberating, to accept this as her fate, that she wasn't free. If it was destiny, then there was still a place for Anna and Jack, and her atonement would be to live elsewhere, with other people, until they both found their way back.

*

Chris still comes round sometimes. Not as often as he used to, when I lived with Jack, and not as often as last year, when I was up in Bounds Green, alone in the post-Jack studio. It isn't that he doesn't like Laura, but he comes to me for the quiet, as much as the talk.

He used to come a lot when Jack and I lived in Muswell Hill. Chris and I existed outside of the standard working week, and there were many hours of quiet we could share, when Jack and Sylvia were at work. Chris's job as a café manager means odd hours and days off midweek, and I was a full-time student at the time, reliably at home except for Monday, Wednesday and Thursday mornings, when I had lectures, and the odd seminar. Sylvia works as a PA in a legal firm and her hours, though not strictly nine to five, are pretty regular, and Jack, despite a degree of picking and choosing afforded by his reputation, is still mostly away from Monday to Friday. Jack is a freelance IT security specialist – a professional hacker, if you ask him; he is hired by businesses to break into their computer systems, find the holes and fix them. He likes fixing things and he is exceptionally good at it, but his real talent lies in taking them apart, identifying the hidden weaknesses that can bring a seemingly sturdy structure crashing down. He can do the same with people. He doesn't do it often, his intelligence is not of the cruel kind, but it's wise to remember that he can.

Chris never calls in advance, he just turns up in the hope that I'll be there. I don't know how many times he's done this and found me absent, but I presume there must have been some. I'm always happy to see him. In the Muswell Hill days it was a simple pleasure, a friend dropping by to lie on my floor and smoke a spliff and talk a little, a welcome break from studying. He'd often time it so we'd have an hour or two alone before Jack returned from work, and then the three of us would crowd the room, drinking tea, before Chris made his reluctant way back home or, sometimes, called Sylvia to join us for dinner. But now, since I left, his undemanding presence carries a different weight. Chris and I became friends because of Jack and although it's been almost a year and a half since we were all together, the link is still there. When Chris comes to see me now, he doesn't come alone.

Chris is a tall man, almost as tall as Jack, and he takes up most of my floor. He's much more comfortable lying on the floor than sitting in chairs or sofas. My bedroom here is perfect, the mattress on the floor serving as his pillow, and the floor itself carpeted, much warmer than the battered, draughty floorboards of my studio flat. It's a small room. I've managed to squeeze a desk in, but that doesn't leave much floor space, and the three of us fill it up: Chris laid out, with his head on the edge of the mattress, and me leaning against the wall opposite with my knees bent so our legs don't cross, and Jack lingering in the corners, never quite settling down. We pretend he's not there, Chris and I; we skirt around him and talk about other things. It's hard not to brush against him, sometimes, no matter how careful we are, and there are times when I get caught on the edges of him, a sleeve caught on a loose nail, but I've always managed to pull myself free with not too much damage done. Always, so far, until today.

There is a period of silence when he arrives, with me against the wall with a cup of tea balanced on my knees and Chris lying down as usual, smoke drifting out of his mouth and up to the ceiling. Every now and again we both lean forward to use the ashtray that I've placed in the middle distance between us, though Chris mostly forgets and drops his ashes on his chest.
 'Sylvia wants to get married,' he tells me when he decides to speak.
 'Oh,' I say. I can't see his face clearly, the way his head is tilted back. 'Do you?'
 'I suppose. It's the next thing, isn't it?'

I shrug, but then I realise he can't see me: his eyes are on the ceiling, like a therapist's client on the couch, with the illusion of confessing his thoughts to an empty room. 'I don't know,' I say. 'Is it? Says who?'
'Chris laughs. 'Sylvia, for one.'
'Fair enough.'
'You know Sylvia: she likes shit done in order. And the thing is, we want to have a baby.'
'Wow. Fuck.'
'Yeah.'
'You want a baby.' I can't imagine it. I can't imagine Chris with a child. I can barely imagine Chris and Sylvia having sex; they never seem to touch each other voluntarily.

Chris blows smoke rings; he does that, I've noticed, when he's thinking, to buy himself some time. 'Well,' he says eventually, 'Sylvia does. I don't mind.'

I can't help myself. 'I'm not being funny, Chris, but are you sure you should be having a baby on the basis that you don't mind?'

'Yeah. No. I don't know. But it's the order of things.' His laugh, this time, is little more than a snort. 'House, marriage, babies. It's happening.'

'It's happening,' I repeat, unable to think of anything else.

'There's gonna be a wedding soon, is all I'm saying.'

'Well then, congratulations,' I say at last.

'Thanks. I'll try to make it fun. No stress. Good food. And we'll have a smoking room somewhere, for the boys. And you, of course.'

I smile at the invitation, but I know I won't be in that room.

'Chris,' I say softly, 'you know I can't come, don't you?' I know I'm treading too close to the edge as I say it, but it has to be said, and it has to be now.

'I thought you might say that.'

'I'm sorry. I wish I could. But you get it, right?'

'I get it.' A smoke ring. 'Sylvia won't.'

'I know. She still hasn't forgiven me for that barbeque.'
I've seen her once since that day, a drink in their local with Chris and Toby that she grudgingly agreed to, but even that's been months now.
Chris doesn't deny it. 'Don't judge her too harshly. She just doesn't understand. Sylvia's never gone through this sort of thing.'
'Lucky her.'
'Maybe. But. She's never been in love.'
'Except with you.'
Chris takes a deep pull on his spliff, pushes the smoke out loudly through his teeth. 'Not except – including. She's never been in love with anyone, including me.'
'Don't be ridiculous!' I protest.
Chris props himself up on his elbows to meet my eyes. 'You can't be that surprised,' he says flatly. And, in truth, I'm not, but I'm surprised to hear him say it, right after marriage and babies. 'It's easier this way,' he adds, accepting my stunned silence as confirmation. 'It is what it is.'

It's Sylvia's tunnel, and she has no intention of crawling out, despite what she says. Instead, she's leading Chris deeper into it, sweet, stoical, resigned Chris who follows her blindly in the dark, as she blocks all the exits with pieces of paper, witnessed and signed, sealing them both in. This is what it is, and I don't understand why he'd choose it. I didn't want to believe it, but I think now that Jack was right, in the way he explained Chris's visits. I was a taken aback a bit when he first showed up on my doorstep on a weekday afternoon; I'd known him for about a year and I'd liked him from the start, but I still thought of him as Jack's friend, not mine. I apologised for Jack's absence and expected him to leave, but he only smiled his lazy smile and told me it was me he'd come to see. And then, for the first time of many, he pulled a thin spliff out of his pocket, lit it up, and laid down on the living room floor, with a cushion off the sofa underneath his head. I brought him an ashtray, made tea, and joined him on the floor, because it felt odd to be sitting at my desk, looking down at him. And that's how Jack found us when he came home, laid out on the floor of our living room, half-stoned and giggling like little girls. If he thought this scene strange, he didn't show it and he didn't ask. He just threw his jacket off, squeezed himself behind me, circled me with his legs and motioned to Chris to pass him the spliff. We didn't talk about it that night, after Chris had left, but months later, when we'd both noticed, too many times, the way his eyes grew a little duller, his smile a little tighter when he stood up to leave, the way his shoulders slumped as he walked out the door.

'He doesn't want to go home,' Jack commented as he locked the door behind him. And then he reached for me, gently but urgently, drew me close, leaving no gaps at all between our bodies, so close that I would have lost my balance if his arms weren't wrapped around me. He pressed his face against mine and we stood there, like that, wordless, for many long moments.

'You and I, it's different,' he said before letting me go, and I didn't ask what he meant. 'Chris comes here to have a break from Sylvia.'

'Do you think?' I said. 'That's sad.'

Jack nodded. 'You know,' he said slowly, with a slight frown, as if trying to process the thoughts as he spoke them, 'my friends are always looking for excuses to get away from their girlfriends. They think it's strange, that I don't. But I never feel the need to be away from you. Why is that?'

I didn't reply. We looked at each other, long and steady, in the best answer either of us could give. I took his hand, or he took mine, and we led each other to the bedroom. Together, different, Chris forgotten.

'Don't,' I said later, as we lay tangled in each other, half-covered by the sheets.

'Don't what?'

'Don't ever be away from me.'

'I won't,' he said. 'I promise. Never.'

Never. He's kept his word, so far.

Chris twists his torso to reach into his back pocket for another spliff, and lies back down, eyes, again, on the ceiling.

'There was this girl once, before Sylvia. I couldn't see her, after we split up. I couldn't have anything to do with her. It was too hard.' He pauses to light the spliff, take the first puff that makes the end glow bright. 'So I get it, I get what you're doing. It's just that...'

'What?'

He raises his head to look at me. 'She broke it off. It fucking hurt, but it wasn't working, for whatever reason. But you and Jack. I mean, why? If it's so hard.'

'Chris. I can't.'

'Yeah, all right, I'm sorry. Forget it.'

But he's still looking at me, his eyes twinkling with something like expectation, or a challenge. I break eye contact, drop my gaze to my lap. 'I think he was cheating on me,' I say, as quietly as possible. These are not words I want spoken too clearly.

Chris sits up abruptly. 'No,' he says. 'Not Boo. Not Jack. Not you. No way, man.'

'I don't know.'

'You know!' He sounds almost angry, his face more animated than I've seen it before. 'And if you don't know, let me tell you: that boy would never hurt you.'

It would make me smile, under other circumstances, this reference to Jack, close to forty, as a boy, from his friend who still thinks of him as one. But this is not a time for smiling. I breathe; it's not as easy as it sounds.

'I don't know,' I say again.

Chris sighs, exasperated, and drops back onto the mattress, holding the spliff high up over his head, like a beacon. I sit with my knees close to my chest, making myself small, holding myself together and, as the edges close in around me, I ask it, the terrible question.

'Did I hurt him?'

Chris takes too long to reply; he blows too many smoke rings before he speaks. 'He misses you,' he says finally. And that's my answer, and it's all edges now, no pulling free this time. The damage has been done.

I stand up. 'Shift,' I tell him, and lie down next to him, claiming a stretch of mattress for my head. 'Give me that spliff.'

We pass it back and forth, taking slow, deep drags and making signals with the smoke that no one outside this room can see, or decipher. We lie there, side by side, each in a tunnel of our own choosing, neither of us understanding; both helpless to help the other out.

'I'm sorry,' I offer at length, a small token for what has passed between us this afternoon; I know we won't talk about this again. 'About that girl.'

'Yeah,' says Chris. 'It is what it is.'

And from the corners, from the edges of this semblance of a life that I've carved out of his absence, where he lingers, Jack nods. True to his word. 'You're still here,' I tell him, in my head. 'Why is that?'

But he doesn't reply.

Five

Robert came along when Anna stopped looking for Jack. When she resigned herself to a destiny and stopped looking for anything at all. Perhaps that was what did it, lulled her into a numbness that felt safe. Robert had nothing of Jack, no context to restrain him, and he just strolled right in.

It was an afternoon in mid-August. Ollie, her boss, rushed in after lunch, with another man in tow. Anna was behind the desk, proofreading flyers for upcoming workshops. She looked up dutifully, nodded to Ollie and smiled at the stranger. He wasn't a client; she'd never seen him before.

'Oh, Anna, good,' said Ollie. 'This is my friend Robert, I'm trying to convert him. Do your thing with him, will you, darling?'

'Yes boss.'

'Jon's teaching beginners' at 2, right? Sign him in with a guest pass, I'll fix it later. I've got a conference call upstairs, I forgot about it!'

'Sorted,' Anna assured him, and Ollie sprinted up the wooden staircase to his office, with a parting wink at his friend.

Robert approached the desk, and thrust his hand out. 'Anna,' he said formally. 'Hello. I'm Robert.'

'Hi,' said Anna, giving the hand a perfunctory squeeze. 'Welcome.' She passed him a form to fill in, and went through the usual questions: had he done yoga before, what was his fitness level, what was he hoping to achieve.

'First yoga class,' he said, 'but I do a lot of weight training. As you can probably tell.' There was pride in his voice, and Anna understood this was an invitation to admire his muscles. She refused to indulge him; she looked up from her screen, caught a glimpse of the snug white t-shirt clearly intended to place those muscles on display, and gave Robert a tight smile.

'I also run,' he continued. 'But I'm stiff. Ollie said yoga might help.'

'Absolutely,' Anna said brightly, and gave him directions to the changing rooms and the studio, where the class was about to start.

'I can touch my toes,' Robert announced, as he was leaving.

'Good to know,' said Anna caustically, before she remembered herself and her position. 'But take it easy today, just enjoy the class.'

She watched him walk down the hallway, took in the swagger in his step and the puffed-out chest, and permitted herself a snort once she heard the changing room door swing shut. She knew his type: he'd approach yoga competitively. She was willing to bet he'd injure himself before long, trying to prove there was no pose he couldn't do. If he came back for another class, which she doubted. Guys like him rarely did.

She entered his details from the form: Robert Kelley, age 29. He lived somewhere not far from her; his postcode was N4. He had left the "Occupation" field blank. She made him a membership card, put it aside, and, after signing in the clients for the 2pm class, went back to her proofreading. She thought no more of Robert.

He must have spent a long time in the changing room because Jon's class had been out for a while and all the students long dispersed before he emerged. His hair, Anna noticed, dusty blond and spiky short with a hint of a quiff, had been freshly and meticulously gelled. He leaned over the desk; he smelled strongly, sharply of deodorant, an archetypal manly scent. He said her name with undue familiarity.

'How was that?' she asked in her most professional tone.

'Easy,' he said dismissively. 'Slow. Not very challenging at all. Maybe next time I'll try a higher level. That class was full of old ladies!'

Anna ignored the last comment. 'That's up to you, of course. But I do recommend sticking to beginners' classes for a bit, until you get used to the poses. Perhaps the challenge for you is to slow down.'

'Perhaps,' he said, unconvincingly, distracted. 'You have a great tan.'

'Oh,' Anna said. 'Thanks.' It was true. Ollie had let her take all her holidays at once, and she'd spent three full weeks in Greece, camping on the islands with Cat and Dylan and an assortment of their friends, making up for the summer before. Her skin, bleached by long-term exposure to the pale English sky, had reclaimed its natural darkness. She'd only been back a week and London had been kind, so it held.

Robert was staring at her a little too intensely, his mouth doing something between a pout and a grin. She found it a bit disconcerting.

'This is for you.' She slapped his membership card on the desk, and picked up the phone. 'I'll let Ollie know you're out.'

He lingered, after Ollie had come down to say goodbye and disappeared back upstairs, muttering about reports. He hovered by the desk, gym bag at his feet, playing with his newly acquired membership card, turning it around and around in his hand as if it held great interest.

'Do you need anything else?' Anna asked politely.

'You have my number,' he said, in lieu of a reply.

'Excuse me?'

'On that form. You have my number. You can call me.'

'We're not allowed to do that,' Anna replied drily. 'Data protection.'

'Right.' Robert arranged his lips into a full-on pout. 'But you could give me yours.'

'I could,' Anna said. 'But I won't.'

'OK.' He smiled broadly, completely unperturbed. He had good teeth, Anna noted grudgingly, a nice smile. 'I'll see you soon.'

He swaggered out, and Anna snorted again at his back, convinced that was the last she'd see of him.

She was wrong. He kept coming back, always in a pair of charcoal grey tracksuit pants and a tight white vest that he had evidently adopted as his yoga uniform, and always lingering at the desk before and after each class. As Anna had suspected, he ignored her advice and shunned beginners' classes for those he considered more advanced.

'What are the hardest classes on here?' he heard him ask Lex one evening, brandishing a printout of the schedule. 'Your colleague refuses to tell me.'

Lex glanced over at Anna, who rolled her eyes. She'd had this conversation with him several times by now, had tried her best to make him see that yoga wasn't about *hard*, but he wouldn't be told.

'I have given Mr Kelley some suggestions,' she said pointedly, 'but he would prefer something more challenging. I'm sure he knows best.' She had taken to calling him Mr Kelley mockingly, in response to his infuriating arrogance that he mistook as charm; instead of taking it in the spirit it was meant, he seemed to like it, which infuriated Anna even more.

'You should listen to Anna,' Lex said diplomatically. 'She knows what she's talking about it.' But she picked up a highlighter and marked some classes on the schedule anyway. Anna sighed loudly and threw her hands up at the both of them, in a gesture of surrender.

'What's the deal with that guy?' Lex asked later, after Robert had signed himself in to an advanced Ashtanga class that Anna was certain would kill him.

'He's an idiot with a yoga deathwish. He's Ollie's mate.'

'He's into you.'

Anna laughed. 'Who, Robert? I think Robert's mostly into himself.'

But he did linger. And he pouted at her, often. He was the first man Anna had met who could pout.

Ollie cornered her a few days later, as they were closing up for the night. Anna was in the process of refilling the stapler when he came and stood next to her.

'What have you done to my friend?'

'I'm sorry?'

'Robert. He keeps asking about you. What you're like, what you do, if you have a boyfriend. You don't, do you? You're single, right?'

Single, Anna thought, not free. 'Yes,' she conceded. 'I suppose I am.'

Ollie grinned. 'Anna. International woman of mystery.'

'I'm not mysterious at all. I just have nothing more to say on the topic.'

'I doubt that very much. But anyway, that's what I told him.'

'Who?'

'Robert! I said I thought you were single. He seemed happy about it. I suspect he's planning to make a move.' Ollie regarded her critically, examining her face for a reaction. It was awkward. She got on with Ollie, but they'd never had this sort of conversation before, and he was still her boss, still Robert's friend. Her answer was careful.

'That wouldn't be such a good idea...'

'No? How would you know unless you try? Open up your heart and trust in the universe and all that.'

Anna put her hands together in prayer and took a bow. 'You are my spiritual guru,' she said, and Ollie winked. 'How do you know Robert?' she added, curiosity prevailing over her determination to remain disinterested.

'Went to school together in Reading, hung out a bit.'

'He's from Reading too?'

'As far as I know. Hadn't seen him for years, we lost touch when my parents moved us over to Essex.'

'You're an Essex boy! I never knew.'

'I am *not* an Essex boy. I just lived there for a couple of years.' Anna smirked. 'I'm not! Show some respect. I can sack you, you know, I'm your boss!'

'Namaste to you too, gentle leader.'

'Whatever. Anyway, Robert moved to London maybe a year ago, sent me an email. We meet up for a drink, on and off, watch a game.' He paused. 'He's a good bloke.'

'I'm sure he is,' Anna replied, although she was nothing of the sort. 'But he's gonna hurt himself one of these days if you don't stop him. He won't listen to me.'

'What do you mean?'

'He went to level 2 Ashtanga the other day. And last night, I caught him in the studio on his own, after class, trying to get into headstand.'

Ollie winced. 'Fool. I'll talk to him.'

'Do. Please. I really don't want him breaking his neck on my shift.'

'Is that a little bit of concern I detect?'

'Yes. Of the professional kind,' Anna said curtly.

'Right you are. Leave it with me.'

The next time Robert came in, he brought a book of poetry with him. He placed it on the desk, right under Anna's nose, as he ostensibly searched for something in his bag. Anna recognised it immediately: it was a Faber edition of Philip Larkin's *Collected Poems*; she had a copy on her bookshelf at home. She was intrigued, but she could sense, instinctively, that Robert wanted her to ask, so she didn't. He left it there for as long as possible, but eventually he had to put it away.

'You told on me,' he stated, as he zipped up his gym bag. He looked at her, challenging; his eyes sparkled.

'Just making sure you practice safely,' Anna replied, unapologetically.

'Well, you won. I've been banned from advanced classes. Today, I'll be going to the intermediate class. Where I will *safely* die of boredom.'

'Excellent choice, Mr Kelley,' Anna said, and swiped him in.

He didn't speak to Anna after class; he merely nodded at her and went straight to the sofa in the reception area, where he arranged himself neatly, legs crossed, and brought out his poetry book. Anna watched him, surreptitiously, immersed in Larkin's verse, his face buried between the covers. She broke; she went over and started tidying up the books and flyers on the coffee table.

'You read poetry,' she said.

Robert lowered the book. 'What? Oh, yes,' he said casually. 'I read a lot of poetry. Does that surprise you?'

'A little,' Anna admitted.

'Well. As a matter of fact, I studied English Literature.' He sounded a bit huffy, defensive, and Anna felt bad: she had assumed he was all about football and weight lifting and generally being macho, and yet here he was, reading poetry after a yoga class. Which said something about both of them.

'I didn't know,' she said, subdued. 'I studied literature too.'

'Yes,' Robert said curtly, as if he already knew. Ollie must have told him, Anna realised. He often teased her about her degrees and how she put them to good use by signing people into yoga classes. 'You don't really know much about me at all,' Robert added. He smiled, but the words sounded like an accusation. He knew because he'd asked. She hadn't; she'd just assumed.

'I love Larkin,' Anna offered, to make amends. 'What's that one with the hedgehog? I think it's my favourite. It always makes me cry.'

Something like irritation crossed Robert's features. He ignored the question. 'I don't have a favourite. They're all good.'

It was the end of the conversation, and there were no more flyers to rearrange. Anna went back to reception, and Robert went back to his book.

He came up to her as he was leaving, the book conspicuous in the side pocket of his bag.

'The Mower,' he said. 'The one with the hedgehog.'

'Yes! That's the one.' She avoided his eyes, which were intent on finding hers. She felt nervous around him all of a sudden. She didn't like it; she wanted him to go.

He obliged her. But he'd only made it halfway to the door before he turned around and strode purposefully back to the desk.

'You could get to know me,' he said. Anna struggled for a response, but he didn't give her time to produce one. He leaned over the counter, grabbed a pen, took out the book and scribbled something on the first page. He closed the cover, and held it out to her.

'Here,' he said. 'My number. Now you can call me. No data protection.'

Anna didn't move to take the book. She wanted to scream at him: for his arrogance, for writing in a poetry book, for how unsettled he was making her feel. He gave her an add look, a pout-frown, and let the book drop on the desk. They both looked down at it.

'But,' Anna stammered, 'don't you want it?'

'You can give it back to me when we go out.'

That's not happening, Anna thought defiantly as she watched him walk out, without another word, his swagger more pronounced than ever. But she was wrong, again. She called him that evening. Her earlier nervousness had settled into an eerie calm.

'Alright,' she said when he picked up the phone, without preamble or introduction. 'Let's go out.'

***

Robert resented being called Rob, or Bob, or any other diminutive or nickname; he thought they were common. He had an issue with things he deemed common, in general, as Anna found out on their first evening out. She also found out that he was, actually, quite charming, when he relaxed and the arrogance subsided; he could be funny and self-deprecating, in a way that was obviously and entirely deliberate, but enticing, nonetheless, and the sarcastic rapport that they'd developed over the past few weeks carried them through that first date and many more after that. It had a vicious edge that excited them both, and as long as they only touched upon it, lightly, and didn't push, nobody got hurt. The sex didn't hurt, either. It hadn't been great the first time, back at her place on the third evening they went out, but it hadn't made her cry, either, and it got better. It was adventurous and a little dirty, a self-serving act focused entirely on pleasure, and it took Anna places she'd never been before. And she let it. She let herself be carried off.

There was nothing of Jack in Robert. Nothing at all. Only the Irish surname, a relic from a great-grandfather, far down the line. There were no comparisons to be made, no measures to hold up against him and find him wanting. Perhaps that was what did it, the lack of context, what allowed Anna to let Robert in without conflict, without considering him a replacement for Jack. Jack could not be replaced. He occupied another place, another tense, the always and the not yet, while Robert roamed free in the here and now.

She had resigned herself to a destiny, but this was a different kind of resignation, because she didn't even know it by its name. She called it love.

*

Chris and Sylvia get married in December, on the day of the Winter Solstice. I receive the invitation in the post and I RSVP that I cannot attend, after calling Chris to thank him. He puts Sylvia on the phone, who accepts my apologies coldly. I tell her that I'd like to go and see them and bring my present, once they're back from their honeymoon in the new year, and she agrees.

I feel bad that I'm not going. Sad, a little angry that it has to be this way. Guilty that I'm letting Chris down. It's going to be a small wedding, just under thirty people, and I'm supposed to be one of them, one of the few they've chosen to share the day. They're having it at the town hall in Islington, and they've hired a venue in Camden Lock for the party afterwards.

'No smoking room,' Chris tells me, sadly, 'but it's right by the canal, so we can always slip out for a smoke. Are you sure you won't come?'

He knows my answer, but it's nice that he asks.

Cat tries to talk me into it, too, enlisting the help of Dylan and arguing that it's different now that I'm with Robert. It's a week before the wedding and we've met for coffee, Cat, Dylan and I. Robert is on the early shift at work and will join us after, and Cat's making the most of his absence. We can't talk about this when he's here. I've mentioned Jack in passing, as if he were a thing of the past; I haven't told him about the wedding, but Sylvia's made my invitation a plus one.

'It'll be fun,' Cat claims, 'won't it Dylan?' The four of us can hang out together, she tells me, and Robert will act as a buffer. 'And I won't leave your side,' she promises, but I don't want anyone between me and Jack in any capacity, not Cat and certainly not Robert.

Dylan's very excited about finally meeting Jack. He's heard a little about him from me, a lot more, presumably, from Cat, and he's attained mythical status, godlike or demonic, depending on how you tell the story. And on the narrator, I suppose. I suspect Cat's telling is leaning towards the latter, because of her loyalty to me and the fact that Jack's been a source of pain; she's chosen to be very unimpressed by him ever since we broke up. Which upsets me, because they're friends.

But then she suggests that Jack and I could be friends, that Chris and Sylvia's wedding could be an opportunity for us to move forward, and it's the most absurd thing I've ever heard. I would laugh if it didn't make me want to weep. The idea of Jack and I in the same room, but separate. Of Jack and Robert in the same room, when separate is how they should always be. The idea of Robert and I in the same room as Jack, my hand in another man's, openly, for Jack to see. I'm not ready to belong to someone else in Jack's eyes, for him to witness such a thing. I'm not ready to confront it myself. I'm not ready for any of this. And I don't want to be Jack's friend. To be friends could only mean small talk and catching up, dipping in and out of each other's lives as if we could spend them apart just as easily as we could spend them together. It could only mean denying what we'd been to each other before, and I went to too great a length to protect that, much further than I'd imagined, to just hand it over now in exchange for friendship.

I try to explain all this to Cat, but I'm rambling, tripping over my own words, because this is fight or flight and I'm trying to do both at once. I know she's acting from a place of love, because she wants the things I've said, at other times, about Robert and being happy to be true; she wants this to work as much as I do. But all she's doing is putting me in a corner, and the intimacy Robert and I have woven in our few months together feels like a veil, hiding my face from the world, a heavy garment that restricts my movements and is making me itch.

Perhaps all relationships are heavy things. Perhaps all relationships are corners and tunnels, after all. Perhaps they rely on limits and boundaries and lines drawn to keep you there, to keep you in your place. Robert seems to think so: he has a very clear idea of what my place is, and he's careful to remind me, nudging me back there, gently but firmly, so I don't stray and get lost. Perhaps that's how it is, and whoever told Jack that we were strange, the way we were together, was right. Perhaps we were wild animals, roaming free in all kinds of landscapes, untethered, spoilt by all that space, and that's not the way people in relationships behave. Perhaps it was just a matter of time before we went feral and turned on each other or, worse, became seduced by the freedom and just wandered off in opposite directions, never to return. Except no: we always returned. We always came back to each other, bringing things to share, trinkets and anecdotes we'd collected from wherever we'd been that day, and the direction of travel was always towards, not away. Like Jack said: we never felt the need to be away. We came back because of the freedom, not despite it. And I don't know how that can be wrong, for all the fences people erect, in the name of security, and the heavy garments they dress each other in. All I know is I don't want to wear Robert's intimacy in the presence of Jack, and if I were to go unveiled, he'd see my face. Everyone would see my face. I can't go.

It's actually Dylan who gets Cat to back down, and promises a full report on the wedding. He squeezes Cat's hand and it's like he's pressed a button, and all the tension that's built up between us just falls away. With a glance at Dylan, Cat lets go of his hand and leans over to put her arms around me. I apologise to her because if I find myself in a corner, it isn't Cat who put me there. I don't want to fight her.

'I'm sorry, too,' she says. 'I didn't mean to push you.' I know she has questions that I'd struggle to answer and, for now, she doesn't ask.

'What's going on?' says Robert, who's just arrived from work. I feel a sting of panic in my stomach, that I might have to explain, but Dylan saves me.

'They're having some sort of girly moment, mate,' he says, making sure to sound both dismissive and slightly mystified at once. 'I'm glad you're here, to even things out.'

I feel extremely grateful to him, even more so when he stands up and gives Robert an awkward man hug. I know he doesn't like him very much; Robert's arrogance, which is his first line of defence in any social situation, rubs him up the wrong way. He hasn't told me, and Cat denies it, but I know.

Robert, a little taken aback by Dylan's unprecedented show of affection, has no trouble at all believing his explanation. I see him roll his eyes at the strange condition of being a girl.

Cat and I release each other, and Robert comes over to claim me.

The day of the wedding is hard. I feel acutely that I'm in the wrong place, and it's a feeling I know well from the days, not long ago, when every place was wrong where I wasn't with Jack. But I haven't felt it since I got together with Robert and it shocks me, because I'd allowed myself to hope it wasn't coming back. It slams into me and knocks the breath out of my lungs, and I gasp for air. Something of this must show on the outside because Robert, who's sitting next to me on the sofa, looks up from his paper with a quizzical expression on his face.

'Are you all right?'

I smile reassurance at him. 'I'm fine. Just a little restless. Want to go to yoga with me? There's a good class on in an hour.'

He shakes his head. 'Nah. I don't think so.'

I don't know why I bother to ask. He hasn't been to yoga for months. He stopped coming soon after we got together. He took one class with me, in the early days, with Joanne, my favourite teacher. I really wanted him to like her, but my enthusiasm seemed to have the opposite effect. I could feel the frustration radiating off him throughout the class, and he was sulky when we came out so I decided, whatever the reason, that I'd keep Joanne to myself. I've only suggested a couple of classes since, and he's said no both times.

'Do you mind if I go?' I ask now. We both have the day off, a rare occurrence, and we're supposed to be spending it together. 'It's only an hour and fifteen.'
'All right. I'll go home, then. Call me when you're done.'
'Let's do something fun tonight!' I say desperately.
Robert leans over and kisses me. 'Let's,' he says.

We get dressed up and go to dinner in a Cuban restaurant on Upper Street. It has garish plastic tablecloths and exotic dishes and two-for-one on cocktails and a dance floor area by the bar in the back. We drink a lot of Pina Coladas and dance and I am over-the-top provocative and turn the entire evening into foreplay. I put all my energy into seducing Robert because the second I stop I'm up in Camden, in a place I've never been but can imagine down to the last detail, standing next to Jack as he plays the part of best man to Chris. I can imagine watching him from across the room as he draws everyone around him into conversation, gesticulating wildly, his voice rising and falling with emphasis, his audience mesmerised. I can imagine the looks he gets from women, sideways glances and open stares, and the bolder ones who approach him, drink in hand or hand on hip, and the way this makes me feel, amused, grateful, a little smug, because he's coming home with me. I can imagine him seeking me out after a while, bumping me with his hip in greeting when he finds me. The two of us sneaking off with Chris and Toby for a smoke by the canal. I can imagine it all as though I'm there, but I'm in the wrong place, and Jack is free to go home with whomever he wants tonight.
    I drain the rest of my Pina Colada, order two more, and whisper breathless, dirty things in Robert's ear as I grind my hips against him.

The report from the wedding is quite brief, and Dylan is acting strangely. He seems subdued, a little awkward around me, and there's something pointed in the way he tells me he met Jack.

'We had a long talk,' he says, and I'm tempted to ask, but Cat swoops in with details of Sylvia's dress before I get the chance.

'She looked beautiful,' she gushes, which is unlike her. She goes on to tell me about the ceremony, the registrar, sombre but friendly, how Chris and Sylvia stuck to the standard vows, the tears shed by both sets of parents, the signing of the book. Sylvia's sister, Juliette, and Jack as witnesses.

'How is he?' I ask.

'Good,' says Cat quickly. 'The same. Jack-like.'

I hesitate before asking the next question: 'Was he alone?'

Dylan twitches visibly, as if he's got something to say, and Cat gives him a look, and the whole thing is only a second or two but I've seen it: he's been silenced.

'What?' I say.

'Nothing. Yes, Jack was alone.' I believe her. Cat wouldn't lie to me about this. But there is something going on. If Cat's terrible poker face didn't confirm it, Dylan does: I look at him, and he turns his head away.

Cat distracts me with descriptions of the party venue, and the food, and the dancing, and how the girl that Toby had brought along was sick on her shoes. Dylan rejoins the conversation gradually, supplying a comment or a missing detail here and there, and retelling a drunken joke that somebody told him. He even smiles at me, and I start to think that maybe I imagined the weirdness earlier, when he says, in a really low voice that is nonetheless heavy with a meaning I don't quite understand: 'You should have been there.'

Cat glares at him, openly this time, but Dylan avoids her gaze and looks straight at me.

'You never really told me what happened with you and Jack,' he says.

I stare at him, dumbfounded. I open my mouth, try to form words, defend myself somehow because I know, without doubt, that this is an attack, but Cat cuts in, and her voice is a knife.

'I don't think this is the right time to talk about that,' she says evenly, and behind the anger I recognise something else: she's protecting me. From what I don't know, but some instinct, some cowardly knee-jerk reaction, tells me to steer clear. I look at Dylan as steadily as I can. 'Sometime,' I promise. 'I'll tell you sometime.'
Dylan holds my gaze for what feels like hours and then blinks, slowly, and gives the smallest of nods. Cat sighs. And we have reached an agreement, the three of us, made some sort of pact that I know nothing about except that the prize, or the price, is Dylan's temporary silence.

***

Chris and Sylvia spend a week skiing in a fancy French resort and return to married life sun-chafed and happier than I've ever seen them. After lengthy negotiations, we manage to find a day that works for all of us, and I go up to visit on a Saturday in late January. I'm apprehensive; it's more than two years since I've been to the house. No one else is invited, I made sure of that, but I know that I'll be greeted by the ghosts of many Sundays, and the cold. Sylvia remains aloof, impassive, as I offer kisses, congratulations and an assortment of little presents, but she softens when I ask to see the wedding photos. We sit close together on the sofa, with the album spread across our knees, and Chris hovering behind us, and she talks me through it. She shows me her soon-to-be husband half asleep and already nervous on the morning of their wedding, her dress, her flowers, her shoes. She shows me the town hall, the waiting room, family and friends in various configurations, the registrar smiling behind her desk. She shows me her wedding day, this one day she stepped out of her tunnel and let the light shine on her, for everyone to see, as beautiful as Cat described, but all I see are photos of Jack. Jack with Chris's parents. Jack with Toby and Chris, their arms around each other. Jack with Chris and Sylvia. Jack fixing Chris's tie. Jack posing with Sylvia's sister, and with a bunch of people

65

I've never met. I thought I was prepared for this, for the impact of seeing him, but I'm not. Jack: the same, a little different. His dreadlocks have grown again, but they're pulled back from his face with what seems to be a ribbon, cream-coloured, to match Sylvia's dress. Strangely enough, this doesn't clash with the rest of his outfit, the clean, straight lines of his deep blue suit, not navy but a duskier hue, the pristine white shirt, the long, thin burgundy tie.

Every photograph is a small explosion of grief, but I'm holding it together until I come to the one where he's signing the book. His hand is poised over the page, but the photographer has interrupted him and he's turned his face to the camera with an expression so serious, eager and uncertain at the same time, as if to say *am I doing this right?* Jack, the most certain man I've met, looking vulnerable. Jack, who's laughed at weddings and ceremonies with me every time we had the chance, who never takes anything seriously, determined now to come through for his friends who've chosen him for their witness, holding the responsibility carefully like that pen in his hand. I feel so proud of him and it's such a redundant emotion because I wasn't there to tell him, because there is no capacity in which I'm entitled to be proud of him any more, and my heart smashes into hundreds of jagged little pieces all over again. There is no slow brimming of tears. They're tickling my chin before I know it, and one of them splashes dramatically, treacherously onto Sylvia's happy memories, which are, thankfully, protected by a plastic sheet. I wipe it with my sleeve and glance sideways at Sylvia, who's staring at me with a mixture of curiosity and alarm. I pull myself together and tap the photograph below, Sylvia and Chris in their first kiss as a married couple, caught in the light pouring in from the windows behind them and glowing.

'You guys look so happy,' I explain. 'I'm sorry I missed it.' I dab at my eyes and smile at her, and she beams back, gratified. She's still in bride land, where people are prone to tears and my outburst, in this context, is not suspicious.

When she excuses herself to go to the toilet there's a creak of the floorboards behind me, reminding me of Chris's quiet presence a second before he speaks.

'I wanted you and Jack as witnesses. I always thought, if there were two people...' He trails off.

'Yeah,' I say, without turning around. 'Yeah. I thought so too.'

He puts his hand on my shoulder, presses down momentarily, and releases, and I want to cry again, but I compose myself when I hear Sylvia clattering down the stairs.

'Come on,' I say, holding the photo album up, 'I wanna see the party!' and she obliges me.

I say goodbye to Chris in the garden, where he's smoking a spliff huddled close to the kitchen door; he's apparently been banned from smoking in the house. Sylvia sees me to the door and I feel like we've mended something, but I need to seal it with some words.

'I'm sorry,' I tell her. 'About the wedding. And that Sunday. I know you were trying to help.'

She hugs me, briefly, and pulls back. 'I was being selfish,' she says. 'You left me.' There's no accusation in her tone, only sadness. 'You were my ally,' and I nod as if I understand, because I know what she's saying, but I don't know why she'd need an ally in me, when it should be Chris, her boyfriend, her husband. I think about my own alliances, and it isn't Robert that comes to mind.

Sylvia shuts the door and I stand on the front step for a moment, and I think about Chris's light touch on my shoulder, and the gentle, welcome pressure of friendship, and the paradoxical weight of absence. I think of Jack, who never dressed me up in anything. I think: not all of them. Not all relationships are heavy. And I think of Robert, waiting for me at his flat, as arranged. I cover up, coat tight around me, scarf up to my nose, hat pulled down over my ears, and go to meet him.

Six

There wasn't much to stay for. Robert was still at the pub where he'd worked since moving to London, close to two years ago, an occupation he described as what he did while "exploring his options" and was always quick to add that he didn't think it was below him, though it was obvious he did. It had never occurred to Anna to judge anyone by what they did for a living or consider them inferior because of it, but Robert's manner when it came to his job, pre-emptively defensive, stirred up some sense of superiority in her that she resented both herself and Robert for. In any case, it wasn't a job to stick around for, and Robert had made that abundantly clear; he had a bright future ahead of him, endless opportunities, and he'd squandered his potential in the pub long enough.

Anna, on the other hand, loved her job. She loved the fact that they were selling the possibility of a better life. She loved the atmosphere, the clients and her colleagues, and she had found real friendship in Lex and Ollie, at a time when she wasn't expecting to make new friends. It would cost her, to walk away from this. But she would, she would consider it, for the sake of a fresh start.

It was too soon, perhaps, for Robert and Anna to need one, only a year into their relationship, but they did. The first few months had rushed by in a blur of sex and excitement and sleepless nights and, for Anna, the profound relief of having found, in Robert, both a distraction and a shield: if thoughts of Jack hadn't left her, at least everyone else had left her alone. Being one half of a couple protected her from the questions, and the double act they performed in public, the witty, sarcastic lines they fired off at each other, often led to comments about how good they were together, and went some way towards easing Anna's doubts when, in the quiet moments, she searched for common ground and found, mostly, empty spaces.

With Anna working in the day and Robert most nights, they didn't get much time to spend together, and they soon feel into a routine whereby Anna would turn up at the pub around closing time and join the staff for after work drinks. In the beginning she'd just hover at the end of the bar, smoking and trying to stay out of everyone's way, waiting for Robert to finish his tasks and pour them both a drink. But as time went by and her presence became unremarkable, she began to lend a hand, bringing in dirty glasses to be washed, wiping tables, putting out ashtrays and menus, rearranging chairs, and when they were done, a little sooner because of her help, she felt like she'd earned her place around the table with the staff, and the drinks that they very rarely paid for. It wasn't long before she was accepted as almost one of them, and included in the – mostly insulting – banter that counted as camaraderie in the pub world. Jared, Robert's boss, even offered her a job, which she politely refused.

'Of course,' Jared had said. 'You're too good for us, with your fancy degrees.' Robert, Anna noticed, looked a bit offended.

This world of drink and darkness was the polar opposite of the one she inhabited in the daytime, and Anna liked the balance it brought to her life. She liked the fact that she could swap leggings and bare feet for jeans and Converse, incense for cigarette smoke, candlelight and chanting for the blinking lights and beeps of the fruit machines and herbal tea for pints of lager. She liked the fact that she could transform from a softly-spoken yogi touting the benefits of meditation to a cynical and sarcastic hard-edged Londoner, who drank beer with the boys and laughed at their dirty jokes.

It wasn't just boys around the table, but they were easier to relate to. The girls, all of them younger than Anna, a couple as young as nineteen, were a tight little group and treated her with suspicion and a hint of competitiveness they didn't bother to disguise. There were two exceptions: a Polish girl called Marta, who had a gentle, quiet manner and an interest in yoga, and seemed to have adopted Anna as some kind of mentor, and Inés, a pretty 22-year-old from Madrid, who had gone out of her way, right from the start, to make her feel welcome. It had the opposite effect: Anna thought friendship should be earned, and had an innate mistrust of anyone who offered it too easily, or too soon; in Inés' case, as it turned out, her mistrust was justified.

Anna didn't have a jealous nature, and she had often watched Jack getting chatted up by women with a smile on her face. Inés flirted with everyone, but it was abundantly clear that she wanted Robert. Anna had found it amusing to begin with: it was too blatant to be harmful, and she was secure enough to not lose any sleep over a girl who had a crush on her boyfriend. But Robert wasn't Jack, and it was obvious he enjoyed the attention. Unlike Jack, who was as much an observer in these interactions as Anna, who'd talk to everyone with the same degree of enthusiasm but never cross any lines, Robert was furtively but actively encouraging. Unlike Jack, who had nothing to hide, Robert was shifty when it came to Inés. But Anna wasn't worried until she made a joke to him about it, about Inés' desperate efforts to get him into bed, and he pretended not to know what she was talking about. Anna, in turn, pretended not to hear the alarm this set off in her head.

She knew long before she was told, but it was Marta who confirmed her instincts were correct. Kind, reserved Marta, torn between her loyalty to her colleague, a loyalty imposed upon her by Inés confiding in her, and her liking for Anna; who had approached her one evening, and asked to speak to her in private. They had gone into the bathroom, ostensibly to make a final check that it was clear of customers.

'I'm very sorry,' she had begun, and Anna knew, but she had to hear it. 'Robert and Inés. They fucked.' She wasn't being vulgar; Marta had arrived in London with very little English, and her classroom was the pub.

Anna nodded slowly. 'How do you know?'

'She told me. I don't know why.'

Anna did: she had told Marta because she wanted Anna to know. She had played on Marta's honesty to get what she wanted, and what she wanted was Anna's boyfriend. Not to fuck him once, but to have him for herself.

'I'm sorry,' Marta said again. 'Are you OK?'

'I'm OK,' Anna replied. 'Thank you for telling me.'

Marta shook her head in obvious distress. 'No. It is not for thank you. It is terrible. I'm sorry.'

'It's not your fault. I sort of knew it anyway.'

'You knew?'

'I had a feeling.'

'Bastard,' Marta commented, and gave Anna a tentative hug.

They came out to much excitement and sniggers and comments about the quality time they'd just spent in the toilet, but Anna only focused on Robert. She didn't trust herself to look around; she couldn't look at Inés.

'I need to talk to you,' she said when she reached him, trying to keep her voice even. Robert put his hand on her hip but she pushed it away. 'Now.'

He followed her outside, through the fire escape in the back, as the boys went 'Oooh'. They stood by the bins, shivering in the cold March drizzle, and Robert did his best impression of casual.

'What's the matter, baby?'

'Did you fuck her?'

'What? No!' And then, as Anna gave a bitter laugh – too late: 'Who?'

'Fuck you, Robert,' she said, taking her time to emphasise every syllable. She watched, with perverse pleasure, as Robert's expression went from indignation to panic to defeat, and his shoulders, always so straight and proud, slumped.

'I'm sorry,' he muttered.

'You're sorry?' Anna squeaked. 'Well, that's OK, then. If you're *sorry*.'

Robert looked baffled. 'Are you being sarcastic? Don't be sarcastic right now.'

'I'll be whatever the fuck I like.'
'But I love you,' he whined.
'Fuck you.' Anna turned to leave, but Robert grabbed her by both shoulders.
'I love you,' he said again, and he actually cried. It didn't make Anna less angry, but it shocked her enough to stop struggling to get away from him. 'Don't leave me. Please. I'll do anything you want.'
'I want you to not have fucked someone else,' Anna said, but she realised she was crying too.
'Please. I'll do whatever it takes. We can get through this. Baby. Please.'

On and on it went, as the drizzle turned to rain, and they cried and smoked and shook with the cold and the tension, and Robert pleaded and Anna shouted, until Jared appeared in the doorway and said he was sorry to interrupt but they were all going home now and could they please come inside and get their things? And Robert and Anna rubbed at their faces and collected their coats and left without a word to anyone, and took the shouting and crying home with them, to Anna's flat, and dragged it out all through the night. And by the morning they had decided that they would give it a go. That Anna would try to forgive, and Robert would try to earn her forgiveness, and ask Jared to make sure he and Inés worked different shifts. It wasn't Anna who asked for this – she wouldn't have – but Robert insisted. He wanted to prove how serious he was.

This was make or break, and it did both. It made them into something they weren't meant to be, and it broke Anna's trust. It kept them together, when they probably should have taken this opportunity to go their separate ways, when fate, by way of Inés, had handed them a way out. It bound them to each other, tighter than their feelings justified, Robert driven by his need not to fail, and Anna by her desperation to make this work, through the word they both used was "love". And in its name they carried on, for days and weeks and months, slow and laborious, dragging behind them a thing that had come to its natural end and had no legs left to walk on its own. This was a relationship past its sell-by date, stale and rotten, but Anna was determined to keep it fresh. It was a McDonald's burger that they were trying to serve up as a three-course dinner, and it was a daily struggle to pretend it kept their bellies full. Perhaps a fresh start, however premature, was exactly what they needed.

***

That's how Cat and Dylan had described it, their vision of what they were choosing: a fresh start. As much as Anna was resistant to the idea, their excitement was infectious. And the thought of London without Cat was almost unimaginable: Anna and Cat had moved here together, right after school, officially to go to university, but secretly and solemnly promising each other they'd never go back. And now Cat was breaking that promise, breaking it joyfully, unapologetically, as if the promise had never been made. Anna was torn between feeling betrayed and wandering whether it was fair to hold Cat to a conviction conceived when they were teenagers. Whether it was fair to hold herself to it.

They had announced it suddenly one evening in October though, looking back, Anna could see that it was planned. They had invited her and Robert over to their flat; Dylan had cooked dinner, and Cat had made dessert – an apple crumble with hot custard – and they had drunk a semi-decent red wine out of proper wine glasses, and then Cat had told them.

'We're moving to Athens,' she said, and her eyes had found Anna's for a moment, before they moved on to Dylan, who reached over to clasp her hand. They both beamed.

'Good for you,' Robert said instantaneously and raised his glass, but Anna was frozen. She could feel Cat's gaze on her again, waiting for her response. It was a while before she could meet her eyes.

'What?' she managed. 'When?'

'December,' Cat replied. 'Just before Christmas.'

'Christmas,' Anna repeated, mechanically.

'I've been offered a job at a private college, teaching history of art.'

'And I'm gonna learn Greek!' Dylan added enthusiastically.

Robert raised his glass again, but Anna glared at him.

'Why?' she said.

Cat shrugged. 'It just feels right. Like it's time.' Her fingers tightened around Dylan's and a look passed between them, fleeting but so intensely private, and Anna understood that it was true: it was time for new promises to replace the old, promises made between Dylan and Cat. It was time to relinquish her hold. She nodded, and it was her, this time, who raised her glass.

'Let's drink to that,' she said.

Robert brought it up again a few days later.

'We could go too,' he said, over lunch at her flat.

Anna swallowed a mouthful of salad, slowly, and put her fork down.

'Go where?' she asked, though she already knew the answer.

'Athens. Couldn't we?'

Anna hesitated. 'We could,' she conceded, 'in theory. But why would we want to?'

'Why not? We have nothing to stay for,' he said, but the *we* that she'd cocooned herself in, that pronoun of safety that she'd longed for at one time, now felt more like a shroud, and Anna wasn't ready to be buried alive. And that inclusive *we* was inaccurate, anyway: Anna had plenty to stay for. She had friends, and friends that had become family; she had the Thames, and Highgate Woods, streets that she'd walked a thousand times and shopkeepers who recognised her and said hello, routines and memories, a past and a future. She had ties that she'd woven painstakingly over the years, ties that she'd laboured for, and that held her in place, in this place that she understood as home.

Robert had none. He had no love for the city or for his hometown of Reading, which he rarely mentioned; he had a vague national pride that was triggered by "foreigners" being critical of his country and manifested as borderline racist comments on immigration, but didn't, apparently, translate into affection. His friendships were transient things, built on convenience and football matches rather than anything deeper. He had no family in the UK; he was an only child, and his parents had moved to Spain when his dad had taken early retirement. It had shocked Anna to find out that he had lived with them, more on than off, until that time, only moving out at age 28 when they sold the house and left the country. No matter how much financial sense it made, the idea of a man choosing to spend his twenties living with his parents did not sit well with Anna, but she kept her misgivings to herself. This, like his job, was a topic that Robert was very defensive about and Anna had learned that defensiveness, with Robert, had a way of quickly morphing into aggression.

'Think about it, baby,' he urged, and Anna flinched, because the word sounded wrong on his lips. She had moments like this, when Robert's terms of endearment still felt over-familiar, the overstepping of a mark, into the place, perhaps, where Jack still dwelt. Robert didn't notice; he was adept at not seeing the things that didn't fit in with his picture of how life ought to be, and that often worked to Anna's advantage – if advantage was the right word for it. 'A fresh start,' he continued, parroting Dylan. 'Doesn't that sound good?'

'I thought London was your fresh start,' Anna retorted, a little more harshly than she'd intended. Again, Robert didn't react.

'London's a shithole,' he pronounced. 'You've said it yourself, often enough.' It was true, she had, but she said it with the affection of a Londoner, a person married to this city, for better and for worse; she was allowed to swear at it, because she did it with love. Like Robert's latent national pride, comments like this set off Anna's defences, and she prickled with resentment at this man who presumed to know London, who dared dismiss it, offhand, after having spent all of five minutes living on its very surface.

But it was true, also, that she was tired. She had grown tired, recently, of this race for survival. She had narrowly missed being on the Piccadilly line train that blew up outside King's Cross in the July 7 bombings that summer; she had grown tired of living in a city that was constantly on red alert, and the casual attitude she, like most Londoners, had adopted towards this only wore her down even more, when she stopped to think about it. It could be good to have a break from this for a while, to walk down a different set of streets, where the sight of a public bin wasn't cause for alarm. And Athens was changing; it was no longer the same place she'd left ten years ago. Perhaps it was time to give it a second chance.

'Are you serious about this?'

Robert looked up from his plate and smiled at her, a hopeful smile, almost timid. And for a moment, a rare moment for a man who starched himself up with arrogance to get through the day, he let his guard down. 'Yes,' he said softly, 'I think so. I could teach English. You could write.'

And in that moment Anna caught a glimpse of a different life, one where Robert taught English and came home smiling every evening after his day of work – work he could be proud of, and where Anna could get back to writing her novel. She saw Athens in the light of a warm, bright sun, a sun you could rely on, and weekend afternoons spent sipping coffee with friends spilling into slow evenings drinking beer under the stars. She saw herself and Robert in a new context, where the promises of happiness could be fulfilled.

She took a deep breath. 'OK,' she said. 'Let's do it. Let's move to Athens.'

Robert stared at her with sparkling eyes. 'Really?'

'Really.'

He stood up and pulled her off the sofa and swept her up into a skipping dance around the living room, holding onto her wrists and jumping up and down, and shouting 'We're moving to Athens!', until they were both a little breathless. They fell onto the sofa, Robert covering Anna with his body, covering her body with kisses and repeating, another kind of breathless now, how much he loved her. And afterwards, when they both lay draped half on and half off the sofa, with their clothes in crumpled piles all around, he propped his chin up on her chest and looked into Anna's eyes.

'My baby,' he said. 'It's gonna be amazing. Just you and me.' And Anna tried not to acknowledge the hot acid of dread that bloomed in her stomach at those last four words, and that pressure she felt on her chest was only Robert, her boyfriend, her love.

'Just you and me,' she repeated, like an exorcism, and brought her arms around Robert's back, and held on tight. The pressure on her chest increased. 'I love you,' she said. And then she cried, and Robert freed one of his arms and reached up to brush her tears away with the palm of his hand, and he smiled at her sweetly because he thought these were the tears that women cried after sex, overwhelmed by emotion, and this was a happy moment.

It's what it looked like: a happy moment. A man and a woman, entangled on a sofa post-sex, on the brink of a new life together, the very picture of the personal pronoun of coupledom. But when Anna said I love you, she wasn't sure if it was meant for Robert or for Jack. She wasn't sure if she was making another promise, or saying goodbye. And when she cried, with her arms around Robert, she cried for the *we* that no longer included Jack, the exclusive *you and me* that made her someone else's, and the continent she was putting between them. She cried because this, more than anything she had done so far, looked like moving on.

*

It's the night of our leaving party, and it's come round too soon. My flat is empty save for a suitcase and a few things I'm leaving with Laura, cushions and candlesticks and my spare yoga mat, so she can keep up her practice when I'm gone. Everything else has been packed into boxes and shipped off to Athens, to my parents' flat, to await our arrival. A new flatmate has been found to replace me, a colleague of Laura's, and she's moving in the day after tomorrow; the day after I leave. It's mid March and London's showing no signs of wanting to let go of the winter, the cold, bitter and hostile, biting into every exposed bit of skin and turning it a sore, angry red, but the temperature in Athens has climbed up to twenty and everyone keeps telling us how jealous they are. Cat and Dylan have been gone for three months already, but they're still talking about how much space they have, for a fraction of the rent; they've organised a welcoming party for us, on the other end.

All my friends are here, scattered around the bar in small groups. Laura and I are the first to arrive, and Robert turns up with his flatmates and Jared, Terry and David from the pub; Marta joins them a little later. Stella is here with her boyfriend, and Lex and Ollie with a few of the girls from work. Toby, Chris and Sylvia come together, and huddle up in a corner, Sylvia on a chair and the boys hovering on either side of her; apart from Laura and me, they don't know anyone else. I introduce them to Robert, and he makes a great production of being overly friendly, magnanimous even, a performance intended to show he knows they are Jack's friends and he's cool with it. It was a different story when I told him I'd invited them; he went quiet and gave me a cold look, and then sulked when I pretended not to notice, and he's overcompensating for it now. Chris, Sylvia and Toby look a bit taken aback, but they respond with handshakes and pats on the back, and the appropriate amount of small talk. I just find it embarrassing.

'He seems nice,' says Sylvia, after he's sauntered off to the pool table for a game with Ollie. Chris nods, a little tersely. Toby says nothing. I am perversely grateful to them for their loyalty to Jack. I don't question where my own loyalty lies; it's one of those things that are best left alone.

How many directions can betrayal take? How far can you stray in one before you need to acknowledge you're doing it? Robert looks good tonight. Being the centre of attention makes me uncomfortable, but Robert thrives on it, and it suits him. It's good to see him like this – happy, confident, excited – but I keep my distance. We exchange a look now and again, a quick kiss when our paths cross, but we spend most of the evening in separate parts of the room. There's nothing strange about this: we're here to spend time with our friends, not each other, but there's more to it than that, and something deliberate in where I choose to position myself in relation to him. Robert's proximity to Sylvia, Chris and Toby is making me very nervous. This is probably unfair to them, because they are my friends in their own right, but tonight they feel like proxies for Jack, and I don't want them witnessing too many displays of affection between my new boyfriend and me. I know it's absurd: I haven't spoken to Jack in three and a half years, and even if they were to tell him about this evening, which they won't, there's no reason why he should care whose hand I now hold, or where he might be taking me. Or whether I keep looking back, at the spot where I left him, trying to make him out in the distance, even as another man leads me away.

The four of us catch up for a while, and then Toby breaks away and heads straight for Lex, who's lingering by the pool table, watching Robert and Ollie abuse each other over their strokes. I raise my eyebrows at Chris, and he laughs.

'Looks like Tobe's developed an interest in yoga,' he says, as Lex demonstrates tree pose with a drink in her hand, and Toby nods eagerly, as if she's just caused the sun to rise.

'Yeah, Lex tends to have that effect. She does wonders for client retention.'

Chris laughs again, and Sylvia rolls her eyes at our juvenile talk.

'What's happened to the latest what's-her-name, anyway?'

'Who, Carly?'

'Maybe.' Keeping up with Toby's women is beyond me, especially now that I don't see him that often.

'It was Tina, actually,' Sylvia supplies. 'Carly was the one before. Neither of them lasted very long.' Toby's inability to settle down with a regular girlfriend is a cause of perpetual frustration to Sylvia. She's been trying to even out the numbers again ever since I bailed on our cosy foursome, but Toby refuses to play along. I wonder how Lex would cope with barbeque Sundays and being invited into Sylvia's tunnel. I wonder what she'd think of Jack, if she met him there, and it stings, so I abandon this line of thought and force myself back to the present. All three of us turn our heads in the direction of the pool table, just in time to see Toby thread his arm through Lex's and lead her to the bar.

'Here we go,' says Chris, and Toby turns around, as though he knows we're watching, and winks.

Sylvia rolls her eyes again, with an exaggerated sigh. 'Hopeless,' she mutters.

'So how's married life?' I ask.

'Good,' they both say. 'The same.' But they exchange a look.

'What?'

Sylvia grins, and lifts her glass in response. It takes me a few seconds to understand what she's showing me.

'Orange juice?'

She nods, and her face breaks into a smile.

'Wow,' I say. 'Guys. Congratulations!' I hug them both. 'How long?'

'Just into the second trimester.' I must look blank, because Sylvia adds 'Fourteen weeks. It's been a bit rough.'

I notice, then, how her slender frame is swathed in slightly looser clothes than usual, and how she's been sitting down all night. Chris lingering by her side, a protective hand on her shoulder or the back of her chair, at all times.

We chat for a few more minutes, about hospital appointments and midwives and birth plans and how much stuff you need to buy, and then I excuse myself and go to rescue Laura, who's surrounded by four of Robert's pub mates, and is casting desperate glances in my direction. As I'm making my way over, I run into Robert, who pats me on the arse proprietarily before skipping off to the bar. I instinctively turn around to check if Chris and Sylvia saw, but they're looking at each other.

Toby comes over later and pulls me aside. He's holding two shots of tequila, a thin slice of lemon balanced on top of each glass. He passes one of them to me, and we drink without toasting to anything. He has a look on his face that I recognise, and I know what's coming.

'Have you talked to Jack?' This is his standard opening line. He always asks, and I always say no. This time, I just shake my head.

'Does he know I'm leaving?'

'Not from me. Do you want me to tell him?'

I shrug, look down at my feet, settle on 'No.'

Toby looks conflicted. 'You should call him,' he says. 'He...'

'He what?'

'Nothing. But you should tell him. He should hear it from you.'

'I don't see why it would make much difference to him, at this stage, where I am,' I say, bitterly, and the irony of these words hits me, full force, when Toby speaks again. I don't know if it's deliberate, but it's like a punch to the stomach.

'He's selling the flat.'

'The – our – his flat? Why? Where's he gonna go?'

'He's moving down South.'

'*South?*' This doesn't make any sense. Jack grew up in Kilburn, and he's lived in Muswell Hill for as long as I've known him. Longer. South is a place he'll visit, sometimes, but he'd never live there. The world has literally been turned upside down. 'Where?'

'Camberwell.'

'What the fuck's he moving to Camberwell for? No one in their right mind ever chooses to live in Camberwell!'

I sound hysterical and Toby laughs, because my reaction would be comical if my heart wasn't breaking. But my heart is breaking and this, too, is absurd. I am moving to another country with another man; Jack is only moving to another part of the city. His life is separate to mine, and it shouldn't matter to me what postcode he lives it under.

'It's the nicer part of Camberwell,' Toby is saying, but then he trails off because he knows that's not the point – even if we were to agree that a nicer part of Camberwell exists.

It matters. Because, for all my talk of separate lives and moving on, I haven't stopped looking back. Because as long as Jack stays where I left him, I can always look back and reassure myself he's still there. His life will never be entirely separate, not finally, terminally separate, as long as I can still picture it.

I can picture it as if I'm there. I can picture the front door, and the way you have to jiggle your key a little to open it; I can picture Jack walking in, wiping his feet on the mat that we bought together in Homebase. I can picture the rooms he spends his time in, though there are certain blanks where my things used to be. I know the angle the sun hits the bedroom at any time of day and the shadows it casts, the intermittent patter of the dripping tap in the bathtub, the way the kitchen smells. I know what he keeps in the fridge, and the clatter he makes whenever he pulls a pan out of the cupboard. I can almost place myself back there, on any evening, waiting in the living room for Jack to come through the door with two plates full of whatever concoction he's put together tonight. Even as I hold a ticket to a new life, I can still put myself back in the old; I can still reach him, as long as he stays where I left him.

I can't picture Camberwell. And if I can't look back, I'll have to look forward, and I'm no longer certain that I will find Jack there.

Toby isn't laughing anymore.

'Call him,' he says, but I won't. I don't. For all the stories I've written about Jack, all the fictional outcomes and resolutions I've tapped into existence, I can't imagine what I'd say.

Seven

Cat and Dylan were right about the space. The flat that Anna and Robert found, small by Athenian standards, seemed like a palace to Anna, who was used to living in tiny rooms baptised doubles simply by virtue of someone having managed to squeeze a double bed into them, and she spent the first few days going from room to room – four separate rooms, all of them theirs – and marvelling at the fact that she could actually miss a phonecall if the phone was ringing in the living room and she happened to be in the bathroom, all the way at the other end of the flat. Robert, who'd spent most of his life in semi-detached middle class comfort, wasn't quite as impressed, but he couldn't argue with the rent, which came to 300 euro per month in total. It had been advertised as part-furnished, which meant it came with a cooker, fridge and washing machine, and nothing else, and for the first few weeks their only possessions were a spare double mattress, a rickety kitchen table, an old pot with a loose handle and a scratched frying pan that they'd begged off her mum, who also gave them a set of cutlery and crockery of debatable taste that she'd got in exchange for coupons earned at the supermarket.

'It's a bit like camping,' Anna had said, but Robert wasn't into camping and couldn't see what she was so pleased about.

Anna's grandmother donated a sofa bed she had in storage, and a trip to IKEA, as soon as Anna's parents could spare the car for the day, provided everything else they needed to get started. The only thing they didn't buy was a bed; they decided to wait until they both had jobs and save up for a middle range one. Anna didn't mind: she actually preferred sleeping on the mattress on the floor, though she didn't share this with Robert, who found it slightly undignified.

'We're not hippies,' he told her sternly one day, and Anna did her best to limit the number of colourful throws she draped over their furniture.

The flat was on the second floor of a 60s apartment block in the borderline rough neighbourhood of Exarchia, once populated by anarchists and junkies and riot police with shields and helmets, and rebellious teenagers like Anna, like tourists to the war zone, and now frequented by trendy twentysomethings who came to play board games in alternative bars and steep themselves in urban culture. To Robert, Anna described their new neighbourhood as edgy and up-and-coming – sort of like Shoreditch – and made only vague references to its recent past, in case Robert decided it was common and took against it.

'I used to come here a lot, in my teens,' she told him, and described evenings spent watching gigs drenched in sweat and half-drowned in cigarette smoke in tiny, airless basement bars. She didn't mention the used-up needles, the riots or the tear gas. It was safe now, anyway, as much as any inner city area can be, and Anna liked its urban feel, the chaos that greeted her when she stepped out her door. It made her feel less cut off from the world, and kept her longing for London under control. Also, due to the scale of Athens, a ten minute walk from their flat would bring them into Kolonaki, city centre home of the Athenian upper classes, all designer stores and overpriced cafes, and if that gave Robert the impression that they lived in a posh area, she wasn't about to disabuse him of that notion. Anything to keep the peace.

Peace was hard to come by. Robert had been very excited about the move – almost as excited as Anna was apprehensive – but the reality of Athens threw him completely. He didn't know the place, or how anything worked, and the subtle cultural differences he kept stumbling upon made him baffled and insecure. He felt that he had to rely on Anna for everything, and he didn't like it. He didn't speak the language and though Anna assured him most people were competent enough in English to understand him, he refused to even try; he put Anna in charge of all exchanges and interactions, and resented her for it. Anna tried to play down her knowledge, and checked her every word and action for anything that he might perceive as condescending or patronising and lead to a row.

'Why did you bring me here?' he said to her one evening. It was the first time of many that Robert conveniently forgot he was the one who'd suggested they move here and Anna chose, on this occasion, not to correct him.

They had just had an argument about buying cigarettes: Robert had gone to the local shop and asked for twenty Marlboro Lights, and the shopkeeper had looked very confused before attempting to give him two full cartons. Anna had previously explained that cigarettes, in Greece, were bought in packs, and only came in one size, but Robert hadn't listened, and Anna had to intervene. She hadn't said *I told you so*, she hadn't said *why don't you listen*; she had, in fact, thought very little of the incident until they got back home and Robert accused her of undermining him and making him look like a fool. She hadn't said *you're perfectly capable of doing that all by yourself*, but it did occur to her that Robert would have actually preferred to pay for twenty packs of Marlboro Lights rather than admit his mistake, and it frightened her. She thought, momentarily, of Jack, of how the funny side was always the first thing he saw, of how he could laugh anything off; of how easy life had been beside a man who never lost his temper. She looked at Robert, whose hold on his own temper was tentative at the best of times and thought the joke was always on him, and bit her tongue. She channelled the most submissive girlfriend she could imagine and chose words to soothe his injured pride.

'This was a mistake,' he said, and Anna didn't say *you're right*, though it was the first thing she and Robert agreed on for some time. 'It's never gonna work.'

'Of course it will,' Anna said brightly. She summoned every last scrap of optimism she possessed and listed, for the first time of many, all the positives and possibilities of the decision they'd made, all the reasons Robert himself had given for leaving London behind. She used words like "transition" and called Robert brave but, even as his expression mellowed and he took the hand she held out – a gesture of solidarity, to invoke the *you and me* Robert put his faith in – she knew that everything she'd just said would be thrown back at her the next time something didn't go his way. That he would hold her accountable for anything that went wrong. That, it seemed, had become her role.

***

It was Anna, not Robert, who ended up teaching. Three weeks after their move, they started asking questions about getting Robert a job in a private language school, and found out he wasn't qualified. It had never occurred to Robert that being a native speaker wasn't enough, and Anna, who knew that, had been given to understand that he had other qualifications.

'But I thought you had a degree in literature,' she said.

'Who told you that?' he snapped.

'You did,' Anna stammered, taken aback by his hostility. She replayed the conversation in her head. 'You said you'd studied English literature.'

'I never said I got a degree, did I?'

'You implied it.'

'You assumed.'

You misled me, Anna thought. You didn't correct my assumption. You showed me what I wanted to see. She thought about the poetry book that had made her look at Robert in a different light, that was basically the reason they were together, and was now nestled among her own, and how all of Robert's possessions were in this flat, and there wasn't a single book in evidence. You see what you want to see. It isn't love that's blind; it's the desperate people who chase after it, who try to summon it out of thin air and thinner excuses.

She didn't voice any of these thoughts. If Robert had played her, it was only because she was willing to be played. And she was still playing now that she knew this had been a game all along, still looking at Robert and seeing the man she wanted him to be, the man he imagined himself to be, because she was one of the desperate people, and love conquers all. She left the room without another word.

It emerged, later, when Robert had calmed down, that he had started a BA in English Literature at Bristol University, but given up halfway through the second term.

'It was a stupid course,' he said petulantly, without elaborating.

He had returned to Reading, moved back into his parents' house and worked in pubs ever since.

'Would you like to go back?' Anna asked, clinging to the picture of Robert immersed in a book of poetry harder than he did.

'Maybe,' he replied, 'one day,' but he sounded flat, like he was reading out of a script. 'It isn't all about *degrees*,' he added defensively, imbuing the last word with profound disdain.

'Of course not,' Anna agreed, and she meant it. But making one up was a problem. It spoke of things that she didn't really want to think about.

What made it worse was that Anna, with her Cambridge Certificate of Proficiency in English, which she'd taken in school, was more qualified to teach English than Robert – and that was without even taking into account her BA and her Masters, which she carefully avoided mentioning in the immediate aftermath of this conversation. As for Robert's prospects of becoming an English teacher, no school would hire him; his best chance would be to find some private clients, but they were hard to come by, and even they were almost certain to ask a few questions about his background and his teaching experience. They consulted the British Council, who advised Robert to take a TEFL course, and even recommended a few, but Robert, after a perfunctory look at the information and a half-hearted search online, declared this option too expensive and a waste of time. Anna tried to talk him round, offered up the rest of her savings to help pay for the course, and conjured up his dream of teaching English and the smiling, fulfilled man who came along with it, but that dream didn't belong to Robert. It belonged to the man of letters persona he'd adopted briefly, and his ambitions were as empty of commitment as his shelves were of books.

Robert gave up, sank into his version of depression, which took the form of a passive-aggressive self pity with frequent explosions of spite, and spent his days on the sofa in his sweatpants, reading about sports in the English newspapers that he bought for four times their UK price from the shop across the road.

***

Anna had thought her receptionist days were over but with Robert pointedly ignoring the job ads she circled for him in the Athens News, the local English language paper, and their money rapidly running out, she visited a newly-opened yoga and pilates studio in Kolonaki, and managed to get a part-time job on the desk. She fell into teaching accidentally, almost without noticing, and by the time Robert found work, three months later, she had at least four or five private lessons each week.

It had begun with teaching Dylan Greek. He'd already taken a beginners' course at the Hellenic American Union and learnt the basics of daily interaction, but when Anna arrived in Athens, he reminded her of the conversation they'd had during their first meeting, and insisted she took over his education.

'I told you then I wasn't qualified.'

'And I'm telling you now you are. You are my teacher. Teach me.' He smiled, and Anna gave in and agreed to try. It was a selfish decision: she had missed Dylan, and his mixture of easy and challenging, with faint echoes of Jack, was the perfect antidote to the sullen, angry silence she lived with at home. It would be good to schedule a couple of hours a week with him, and finding ways to teach him Greek could provide some of the intellectual stimulation she sorely missed. She also secretly hoped that seeing more of Dylan, outside of a social context, might inspire Robert to get off the sofa and follow his example. Dylan had come to Athens as much a stranger as Robert, but had been proactive, from the start, in finding ways to belong. In just a few months, he had ingrained himself in the expat community, and found work as an electrician in homes all across the city. He was now even starting to get some Greek clients, who'd heard about him from their international friends. The fact that his Greek was poor and consisted, mostly, of quotes from Homer didn't stop him. Perhaps Robert would see this and find some hope; perhaps he'd even join their lessons.

Anna did some research but she found the books used for teaching Greek to adults irritating and unrealistic. She devised her own teaching method, based on the things Dylan was likely to encounter in everyday life, rather than on inane conversations that took place in theoretical situations in fictional airports and tourist sites. She started by teaching him the alphabet and instructed him to invest in a good dictionary, so he could look up any words he came across and know how to pronounce them. They listened to Greek rock songs, pausing them over and over again until Dylan had learned the lyrics; they read food cans and flyers posted through the door and street signs, they watched news and sports' programmes on TV and eventually moved on to short newspaper and magazine articles. And it worked: Dylan was learning through real things that interested him, and he was able to put his new knowledge into practice straight away, and Anna, who'd never had any aspiration to teach, began to enjoy it. So when a colleague of Dylan's approached her, a plumber from Romania he'd met while rewiring a flat in the northern suburbs, and asked if she could use the same method to teach him English, she said yes.

'Dylan's improvement is incredible,' he'd said, his own Greek heavily accented but fluent. 'I've taken English lessons before, and it's never worked. Maybe this time it will.'

Word of mouth and Dylan's tireless PR campaign took over from there, and soon Anna had enough students – most of them Greeks and immigrants from the Balkans learning English, and a couple of British expats wanting to improve their Greek – to consider giving up her reception job. But she held onto it. Though the atmosphere at the studio wasn't quite a serene as Anna was used to, and Athenian yogis were somewhat less evolved than their London counterparts, being there still put her in touch with people she could relate to, and with a part of herself that she needed, now, more than ever. Besides, it was only three days a week, and it entitled her to free classes.

Robert had joined her lessons with Dylan briefly, but it became apparent, as early as the first session, that it wasn't going to last. He resented being corrected or told what to do; he competed with Dylan and even, absurdly, with Anna, and argued with her on almost every point. One time, during the second lesson, he actually threw his pen across the room. Dylan had tried to keep things light by making jokes, but Anna could tell he was losing his patience. Robert's increasingly begrudging participation in their lessons wasn't doing any of them any good: it was disrupting Dylan's learning, and all Robert got out of it was frustration, and when he finally dropped out, halfway through the fourth attempt, and took himself off to the bedroom to sulk, Anna was relieved.

'You made me feel incompetent,' he told her, once Dylan had left and Robert had roused himself from the bed in a combative mood. 'You showed me up in front of Dylan.'

Anna told herself that this was insecurity speaking, not Robert, and that narrowed-eyed glare he was giving her was only an indication of how vulnerable he felt. She fought her instincts and made herself soft: she apologised to Robert for inadvertently upsetting him; it was the last thing, she said, that she wanted to do. She assured him that he was more than competent, that he could do anything he put his mind to.

'I believe in you,' she told him. She implied that it was, perhaps, her teaching skills that were at fault, and suggested he take the Hellenic American Union course instead, and put his education in the hands of the professionals.

Peace. Short lived, because Robert wasn't done.

'Isn't it a cushy life you have, with your yoga and your teaching,' he remarked bitterly. 'It's all worked out for you, hasn't it?'

But Anna had been walking a line on the very edge of her empathy, her desire to be understanding, and this pushed her over.

'Actually, Robert, no,' she said slowly. 'I didn't come here to be a teacher and a receptionist. I'm doing it because I have to, so I can pay our bills while you feel sorry for yourself and read the papers.' She saw him bristling, saw his clenched fists and the spark of anger in his eyes, but she didn't stop. 'But I'm supposed to be a writer. I came here so I'd have more time to write, and I haven't written a single fucking thing. So no, it hasn't really worked out for me.'

She walked out of the bedroom and straight out of the flat and kept walking until she reached the grounds of the Athens Academy, a place where she could normally find some peace, and when that didn't work, she followed the road all the way to Parliament, where the sight of the pigeons and the National Guard did nothing to soothe her either, so she walked on, all the way to the outskirts of Pagrati, and rang the doorbell to her brother's flat.

'My boyfriend's an arsehole,' she said when he opened the door, 'and I left without my cigarettes.'

And George, being a 32-year-old man with no particular desire to discuss his sister's relationship troubles, passed her his cigarettes and a beer, and played her the latest songs that he'd discovered, intervening frequently to draw her attention to a particular guitar riff or a lyric that was coming up. Anna smoked half the cigarettes in his pack, lying on his floor with her legs up the wall, and let the music and her brother's enthusiastic interjections carry her away. She left as it was getting dark, with some change from George for the bus.

'Are you alright?' he asked at the door.

'I'll be fine.'

'I can go big brother on him if you want. Beat him up a little.' He pursed his lips and flexed his biceps.

'I'll let you know if it comes to that.'

Robert was in the living room when she got home. It seemed like he had tidied up and, judging from the smell of garlic drifting from the kitchen, perhaps even cooked. He was out of his sweatpants and wearing jeans, and he looked up slowly when she walked in, hands clasped in front of him and resting on his knees.

'I'm sorry,' he said.

Anna shut the door behind her and stood in the hallway.

'Come here. Please.' He laid his hand on the space next to him on the sofa. Anna took a few steps into the living room, but continued to stand.

'I'm sorry,' he repeated. 'I know you work hard. It's just that I'm frustrated.'

'I know. But you can't take it out on me like that. It's not fair. I'm not doing any of this against you.'

Robert nodded. 'I'm gonna get a job,' he said. 'Take some pressure off you, so you can start writing. OK?'

'OK.'

Anna sat down next to him then, placed her hand on his knee. Carefully, tentatively, Robert brought his arm around her and eased her head onto his shoulder.

'I love you,' he said. 'I cooked you dinner.'

'Wow! I should storm out more often.'

But Robert tightened his grip on her. 'No,' he said. 'Don't do that. Don't leave me again.'

A few days later, Anna summoned up her courage and dug out the manuscript of her almost-finished novel, two hundred and ten pages of it.

She held out this bundle, like a baby, to Robert.

'My novel,' she said. 'Do you want to read it?'

'Of course,' he replied, but he made no move to take it from her hands, so she placed it down on the coffee table.

'It's missing a few chapters. But hopefully, by the time you get to the end of this, I'll have started working on it again.'

'Great,' Robert said. He smiled up at her, and went back to his paper. At least, Anna noted with relief, it was the Athens News. Perhaps he'd started looking at the job ads.

On a whim, she emailed Dylan a selection of her Jack stories, the ones she'd only shown to Laura so far.

In case you still want to read my stuff, she wrote.

Thank you, Dylan replied, within moments. And later, that very evening when she came home from work: *I read them all. Couldn't stop. You are extremely talented. What the fuck are you doing? These should be published.*

She smiled at her screen.

'What are you smiling about?' Robert asked.

'Oh, nothing. Just a joke somebody sent me.'

Her manuscript, she noticed, was still on the coffee table, where she'd left it that morning. Its pages unruffled, untouched.

*

I'm supposed to be a writer. I'm a writer who doesn't write. But it's not true that I've written nothing at all: I've been writing down the dreams. I write them down in a small red leather notebook that I keep hidden at the back of my desk drawer.

Jack and I in a café, stirring sugar into our lattes. There are several chairs around our table, but we sit together on a small sofa, pressed into each other, shoulder to knee; our hands stay on our coffee cups. He turns his head to look at me, and winks.

Jack and I on another sofa, somewhere. My head rests on his shoulder. We both have our eyes closed. We say no words. We just sit.

Jack and I in bed, sitting up. Fully clothed, holding hands. Silence. I turn my head to look at him, and smile.

Jack and I in bed, lying down. There's a thin strip of distance between us, but our feet touch. We keep our eyes on the ceiling, except when we both turn our heads to look at each other. I reach for his hand.

I think the dreams come because I've stopped thinking of Jack. I've trained myself not to think about him, to survive. I've learned, finally, to live without him; not the life I imagined, but a life, nonetheless. I've learned to live with him pushed down, with layer after layer of my new start carefully laid out on top. But with these dreams, he pushes back, and that flimsy construction collapses every time. And what's worse is that it barely makes a sound: it's not substantial enough for that. And still, every time, I build it up again from the ruins, using the same hollow materials that failed me the time before.

It's like trying to hold back the tide with sticks and rocks and feathers and then being surprised that it's all swept away when it comes, as it always does; all my barriers washed away like flotsam, the worthless wreckage of a sinking ship that's taking me down with it. And I'm happy to go, because down there I meet Jack. They are inevitable, these dreams, like the tide. I understand that now: they cannot be stopped. They come roughly once a month, give or take a few days, without fail. Like the tide, they have a cycle, frightening in its regularity. I'm learning to expect them, anticipate them even, but still they surprise me, every time. Accepting a fate isn't easy, even once you've seen it for what it is. Especially then.

This is a good life I have. It's not a charade, exactly. But I live it with a secret, and that's why the dreams come: to remind me. Wordless, they come to show me what I long for, what I miss the most: to just sit with Jack, in silence. They take me there, briefly, for a few moments every month, more vivid, more real than anything I do in my waking hours of living a dishonest life in earnest.

The next day after each dream belongs to him completely. The next day I rise up, gasping for air. The next day I wake up in bed with the wrong man, the wrong, legitimate man, who has claimed his space beside me in sleep, but has no place in my dreams. The next day is given over to Jack, and everything is a charade, and then the tide draws back, and the cycle begins again, anew.

I never appreciated it, what it meant: to just sit. In silence. Without words. I never understood its rarity, its worth, until I stood up and walked away. I never knew it until now, when I only have the words. If I had known it then, if I had known about the inevitability, would I have sat back down, in silence, and waited it out? The next day is always the same: the pain, the longing, the sense of being ripped from the place I belong always the same as the day I walked away. The love, exactly the same.

It isn't over, and that's what I have to live with. That's the secret I keep in this good, new life of mine, when I have learned to live without Jack. My dreams, in a small red notebook hidden in the back of my desk drawer, where my real life carries on, despite me.

Eight

Robert did not find work through the job ads in the Athens News; he found it through Dylan. For a man who often complained how hard things were for him, so much harder than for other people, this came surprisingly easy. He did not have to look for it. He did not have to dress up and go for an interview, agonise over the words the interviewer had used or the way he had said goodbye, or bite his nails through hours of waiting for the call that would determine his fate. All he had to do was drink in a bar and this job, like a cheap woman, had marched straight up to him and sat on his lap. And just like that, Robert was a barman again.

It was an international sports bar at the foot of the Acropolis, run by Dave and Jimbo, two brothers from Leeds with thick Yorkshire accents and a sharp business acumen: they had stumbled upon a gap in the market when, passing through Athens on the way back from a holiday in Ios, they had discovered there was nowhere in the city to watch a game and have a decent pint, and stepped in to fill it. That was three years ago, and their bar was now the Athens expat community's best kept secret: a place to escape to for drinks, networking and a break from the madness that was life in the Greek capital. It showed English football matches and the Six Nations rugby and NBA games and the NLF Super Bowl. It had a jukebox like the ones that disappeared from British pubs sometime in the late nineties, converted to take euro coins, and a DJ on Friday and Saturday nights. It was the only place in Athens that offered Guinness on draft, as well as several interesting lagers, bitters and ales. It served a range of fried and battered bar snacks, imported Salt & Vinegar and Cheese & Onion crisps for the nostalgic, and selected staples of British pub cuisine, such as bangers and mash, steak and kidney pie and a full English breakfast at the weekends, and attracted expats from all over the world and all over the city. To Robert, it was heaven.

Dylan had met Jimbo when he replaced the fuse board at his friend Andy's flat. Jimbo had stopped by for a coffee and a game of backgammon; he watched Dylan as he worked, and told him he might be in the market for an electrician to take care of things at his bar, as he suspected the current guy was overcharging. They exchanged business cards, and Dylan and Cat went to check out the bar the following weekend. A fifteen minute stroll from their flat in Thisseio brought them to the aptly named Sports Bar, so proclaimed by the blue neon sign over its door, but inside it was done up like a typical English pub, and Jimbo greeted Dylan like an old friend and offered him and Cat a drink on the house. They pulled up stools and spent the evening chatting to Jimbo and Dave at the bar, which culminated in the four of them bonding, Greek style, over shots of tequila. Soon Dylan began doing odd jobs for the brothers, and made a point of stopping by the bar at least once a week, to pick up new clients.

'Much like a whore,' he told Anna and Robert happily, when he invited them to join him and Cat at the Sports Bar on a Saturday night. It was shortly after Robert had quit their Greek lessons and though Dylan had said nothing, Anna suspected the timing wasn't accidental. Whether or not Dylan knew it might lead to a job, bringing Robert into the expat community, showing him that there were many others like him out there and they were all, by and large, making it work, could only be a good thing.

It made Anna happy to see how his face lit up as he walked through the door: here, finally, was a place he understood. Dylan led them to the bar and introduced them to Dave and Jimbo, and as soon as Robert settled down with a pint of Guinness in front of him, rivulets of condensation trickling down to the matching beer mat, he was transformed. As if he'd pulled a mask off, the slit-eyed, hard-featured man with the twitching temples and the tight jaw that Anna had been living with for months disappeared to reveal a face that she recognised, vaguely, from a long time ago. The eyes were wide and animated, the forehead uncreased, the lips, soft and full, framing a set of perfect white teeth; the bitterness that he'd been cloaked in fell away, and his shoulders straightened. The change was so extreme that Anna did a double take.

'There you are!' she said, without meaning to, and Robert looked perplexed but smiled at her, nonetheless. He smiled a lot that night.

Anna, who'd ended up sitting between Robert and Dylan, dragged her stool over to the far end, next to Cat, and left the men to it. It wasn't just to give Robert space to be himself, now that he seemed to have remembered who that was, and to talk football and beer and whatever else it was that men talked about, unhindered by the need to include his girlfriend: after months of acting as his interpreter, his advocate, his proxy in all situations, of never leaving his side in case he felt abandoned, of never speaking Greek in his presence, even with her oldest friends, so that he didn't feel left out, Anna, too, was ready to be herself again. To put down the heavy mantle of responsibility that Robert had insisted she carry, and slump in her chair and sip her drink and talk to her friend, in their own language, without the nervous glances in Robert's direction that had punctuated their every conversation since moving to Athens. Spontaneously, she threw her arms around Cat, who looked taken aback for a moment before returning the hug.

'I think it's gonna be alright,' she told her, and Cat smiled contentedly and said 'of course it will be', with the simple nonchalance of someone who already knew that it was. They both turned to look at Dylan, who was, at that moment, leaning over the bar, in the process, inexplicably, of patting the top of Dave's head. Dylan, whose loose curls and strange eyes still made Cat a little woozy, if the smile on her face was anything to go by. Who'd treated his own transition into Athens life like a rollercoaster ride that he shared with Cat, strapped together in their creaky car and screaming with fear and excitement as the world turned upside down and righted itself again. This, Anna thought, the way Cat and Dylan had with each other, was another example worth following. She pointedly, deliberately, did not think about Jack.

It was a good night, and when Anna and Robert got home, a little drunk, they made love for the first time in weeks, and it was slow and gentle and uncomplicated like it had never been between them before. And when Anna cried afterwards, it was because she felt something like hope.

Robert went back to the bar the next day, for a fry-up and a read of the Sunday papers, while Anna was at work. He went back a couple of evenings later, with Dylan and a crew of assorted workmen, who'd just finished a big job in a newly-built flat. He went back with Anna the following Friday and again, on his own, on the Saturday (Anna went out to dinner with her parents and George), and when he returned that evening, he announced that he had been offered a job.

'That's fantastic!' Anna said and kissed him all over his face.

'Really? You're not disappointed? That it's a bar?'

'Why would I be disappointed?'

'You wanted me to be a teacher.'

Anna laughed. 'I only wanted you to be a teacher because I thought that was what you wanted. I don't give a shit what you do, as long as you're happy.'

'Really?'

'Really. How can that surprise you?'

'Well.' Robert looked uncomfortable. 'This is new to me, that's all.'

'There's nothing new about it; it's how it's always been. But,' Anna said, realising, 'you don't feel that way about me, do you? It isn't vice versa.'

'What? Yes! I do! It is!'

'No,' she said gently. 'You look at my successes as your failures. You can't be happy for me. You see it as a competition.' Her voice came out flat, defeated. This wasn't something she knew how to fix.

'I don't!'

Anna looked at Robert, straight in the eyes, for a long moment, and she saw what he was struggling with. She saw the conflict between who he was and who he wanted to be, the potential that was always just out of reach. She saw the two of them forever following that dangling carrot.

'I'm going to bed,' she said. 'Congratulations on your job.'

He didn't try to stop her.

Later, when he shuffled up to her as she lay with her back to him, facing the wall, he told her he was sorry.

'Of course I want you to be happy. You can't doubt that.'

'I don't. But I'd like you to be proud of me sometimes.'

'But baby, I am. I'm so proud of you! I'm always telling people about you!'

'Maybe you could try telling *me*.'

'I will,' Robert said decisively. 'I'll do that.' And then, solemnly, after a pause: 'I'll try to be better. I'll try to be the man you deserve.'

But this, well intentioned as it was, did not give Anna any comfort; it sounded too complex, too convoluted for such a simple thing. She sighed, and let Robert thread his arm underneath her neck, and pull her closer.

'This is our fresh start, now,' he whispered into her hair. 'This is when our new life begins.'

The carrot dangled. Anna closed her eyes.

***

And so it happened that their new life began with Robert working in a bar and Anna at the reception desk of a yoga studio, much like in the old. Like in the old, Anna did yoga and sold monthly passes and discussed the benefits of positive thinking and the use of crystals to unblock the chakras, and Robert served drinks and learned how to mix cocktails and watched football and drank beer after work with the boys. And two, maybe three evenings a week, after the last class at the studio or her last lesson at home, Anna changed into her jeans and went to the Sports Bar, to sit on a stool at the end of the bar by the till, and watch Robert pull pints and drink shots with the customers. She didn't often stay until closing time. Greek bars have a very loose definition of opening hours, and it wasn't uncommon for Robert to come home at three or four in the morning, especially at the weekends. Anna regularly went to bed alone. But when he did make it home in time to say goodnight, he came through the door with a smile, and if he wasn't exactly proud of what he did, he seemed to have at least let go of the idea that he was wasted as a barman, and for that Anna was grateful. A tentative sense of contentment pervaded the little things of their everyday life.

To keep the good feeling going, Anna decided to surprise Robert with a bed; he had started to complain, recently, that lowering himself onto their mattress every night and getting himself off it again in the morning was hurting his back. Besides, with her income from the studio and her private lessons, Anna was earning enough, now, to be able to afford such gestures. She picked a day when she was off and Robert was at work, and talked George into coming along to help her, and together they drove to IKEA and bought the least bohemian, most minimalist bed Swedish design had to offer. It was plain, black, very sturdy, and had sensible storage drawers on the side, and it weighed a ton. It came in two boxes, and it took them forever to load it into the car and then carry it up two flights of stairs to Anna's flat, and then they spent what felt like days assembling the thing while keeping up a constant stream of bickering. George was meticulous in his approach and insisted on reading the instruction leaflet from cover to cover before even taking the parts out of the boxes, while Anna was itching to get started, impatient for the gratification of seeing it come together. They were rude to each other as only siblings can get away with and Anna fantasised, several times during the assembly process, of whacking George over the head with one of many identical looking pieces of wood that he seemed, miraculously, to be able to tell apart.

When they were done, they both took a moment to admire their work, but although they stood together at the bedroom door and looked at it from roughly the same angle, they each saw entirely different things. George saw a bed, and a job well done; Anna saw a symbol. This was the first major piece of furniture that she'd bought herself: a double bed for a cohabiting couple. It felt more grown up than anything she'd done before; it felt like settling down and, as she turned this around in her mind, the word "down" fell away, and left only settling. Something urgent and unpleasant stirred inside her, something like panic, except a little duller, and she experienced, for a moment, the same sense of displacement that often came in the aftermath of her Jack dreams.

She made coffee and she and George took their mugs into the living room and sat at opposite ends of the sofa, with their feet up on the cushions.

'Should there be some sort of certainty?' she asked when they were both on their second cigarette.

'What do you mean?'

'Like, when you're with someone, long term. Shouldn't you feel certain?'

George sighed. 'What's gotten into you?'

'I don't know. This – ' she swivelled her head to indicate her flat, her life with Robert, 'it's all very serious. And it's nice. But forever?'

'I doesn't have to be forever. Forever is a scary word.'

'Yes, but isn't that the point? To not be scared of it?'

'I guess. But I'm no expert. The closest I got to forever was with Ingrid, and that was only three years.' He paused. 'I think we always have doubts, to an extent. It's natural. We're always thinking there could be something better around the corner; that we might be missing out.'

'But what if the better thing has already happened, and you did miss it?'

'Then you're fucked,' George said, with a sardonic smile. Anna started to laugh; at least, she thought it was laughter that she felt rising up, but it didn't turn out that way.

'Oh!' George reached over with his foot to nudge her gently on the shin. 'Why are you crying? What is it? You have doubts about Robert?'

Anna nodded desperately and made a whimpering sound as she tried to hold back a sob. George, she knew, was uncomfortable with crying.

'Well, you haven't signed a contract. You haven't done anything that can't be undone.'

But Anna wasn't so sure, and these words of comfort only brought her fear into sharp relief. She wiped her face, clumsily, with her hands, and took a deep breath.

'You know how people say that when they meet the person they're supposed to be with, it feels as if that part of their life is sorted? Like it's done, and they're free now to get on with everything else?'

George shrugged.

'That's certainty,' Anna continued. 'I don't feel that. I don't feel free. But I felt it before. With Jack.'

'But you left him. It didn't work out.'

'Yes.' Anna hesitated to say the next words out loud; she mumbled them, head bowed, eyes on her lap. 'But what if I made a mistake? What if I wasn't supposed to have left?'

She looked up at her brother expectantly, almost certain he'd dismiss this with his usual cheerful cynicism that would never accommodate the idea of things that were and weren't supposed to happen. That he'd assure her that she couldn't have made a mistake of such magnitude; that he'd tell her she had done the right thing, even though he had no way of knowing. He didn't. He just held her gaze, blinked slowly, and said nothing.

'What? What are you thinking? I'm fucked?'

And George smiled, but it was a smile of sympathy this time. 'You're fucked,' he confirmed. 'If that's the case, you're well and truly fucked.'

And this time Anna laughed properly, this simple, grim verdict flooding her with a curious, hysterical relief, and George, after a nervous glance in her direction to ensure she wasn't about to start crying again, got swept up in it and they both laughed until their ribs hurt and they had tears in their eyes.

'We need Joy Division,' George pronounced once he had caught his breath. 'Do you have Joy Division?'

Anna rolled her eyes. 'Of course I have Joy Division.'

'Love will tear us apart,' George clarified, unnecessarily, as if it could have been any other song.

Anna cooked George dinner to thank him for his help with the bed and when he went home, a little after midnight, she settled on the sofa with a book to wait for Robert. She had been drifting in and out of sleep for a while when he returned; she heard him shuffling up to her, felt him sit on the edge of the sofa, and she opened her eyes.

'Hi baby,' he said, bending down to kiss her.

'Hi,' Anna drawled sleepily. 'You OK?'

'Knackered. Why aren't you in bed?'

'I have a surprise for you,' she replied, rising to her feet and pulling Robert up by the hand. 'Come.'

She led him to the bedroom and let him take in the sight of the new bed.

'You did this?'

Anna nodded happily. 'For you.'

'You're amazing!'

'George helped,' she added loyally. 'George did most of it.'

Robert flung himself on the bed, rolled around experimentally. 'Nice,' he said, propping himself up on his elbows.

'You like it?'

'I love it.' He looked at Anna with a glint in his eyes. 'Suddenly I'm not so tired anymore. What do you say we try it out?'

Anna raised her eyebrows in response. 'I'm not sure I know what you mean.'

'Come here. Let me show you.' He opened his arms and Anna slid into them.

Afterwards, as they lay, drowsy and contented, on their new bed, Anna decided to do as the magazines advised, and share her fears with her partner. She peeled her head off Robert's shoulder, and placed her palm on his chest. His eyes were closed.

'Robert?'

'Mmm.'

'Do you ever get scared?'

He opened his eyes and looked at her, slightly unfocused. 'Of what?'

'All this.' She traced a line down his chest, down to the dip of his solar plexus. 'You meet someone, and there are two ways it can go: you either break up, or you stay together forever. Doesn't that scare you?'

'Which one?'

'Both, I suppose.'

'Sure,' Robert replied, a little too easily. 'But I don't think about it all that much.'

'But do you see yourself with me forever?'

'Sure,' he said again, and stifled a yawn. 'Why not?'

'It's a long time. Don't you have doubts?'

'Not really.' His eyelids fluttered, and his lips formed a loose smile. 'Not at all.'

But we always have doubts, that's what George had said. And here was Robert claiming he had none, and hearing none in Anna's questions. And there was another thing, a contradiction that she'd kept to herself: not always. With Jack, there had never been the slightest doubt in her mind.

'Robert,' she whispered, 'do you believe in fate?'

But he had fallen asleep.

***

While Anna learned to come to terms with her double bed, Cat and Dylan took serious to the next level, and decided to get married. It made Anna laugh, because Cat had always been openly and vehemently opposed to marriage, even more so than Anna herself, and they had both made big statements about how they'd never do it. Anna had been fully prepared to drag this out as long as she could, but Cat's explanation, when confronted, was too perfect to spoil with jokes.

'That was marriage in the abstract,' she said, without a trace of shame. 'But I'm marrying *Dylan*.'

Anna liked that she chose to tell her alone, without either Dylan or Robert present. It felt like a moment of some significance, of some density that shouldn't be diluted, spread out too thin among too many people, and she was moved that Cat also saw it that way. The moment belonged to Cat and Dylan, and they belonged to each other now, but Cat had given her a part of it, a token, perhaps, of all the years when they had been each other's only constant, getting each other through, so they could end up here, so that this moment could exist. And maybe, too, a promise, that Cat and Dylan did not cancel out Anna and Cat. A reassurance that Anna needed more than she'd want to admit, at this time when, in the name of a shared life, she felt like she was giving up more and more of the things that had once belonged exclusively to her. She missed her friend. Though Cat and Dylan as a couple were almost as easy to be around as Cat on her own, and Dylan never complained, as Robert did, if the two of them sometimes forgot themselves and drifted into Greek, it was still not the same as having Cat to herself. Time with Cat alone was like coming home to her most familiar childhood room, surrounded by her old, worn-out and beloved things: she knew who she was in there; it was a place where she'd always be accepted, without any questions asked.

Cat called to make a plan.

'Let's go out,' she said. 'Just the two of us. Tomorrow night?'

'Yes please! Pick me up from work? I finish at eight.'

Anna made an effort: she put a skirt on over her leggings, and ran some mascara through her lashes. She rarely went out these days, except to the Sports Bar when Robert worked, which didn't count. This felt like an occasion and, bizarrely, as she waited outside the studio for Cat to collect her, almost like a date. She told Cat, who laughed, and promised her a very romantic evening.

'Perhaps,' she added diplomatically, 'Robert needs to take you out a bit more often.'

It was November, but it was still mild enough to sit outside, and the wine helped to keep them warm; Cat had insisted on buying a bottle of red for them to share.

'So, Dylan and I are getting married,' she said, without any preamble, as soon as they sat down and their glasses were full. She said it so matter-of-factly that it sounded nothing like an announcement, and Anna fell into stunned silence as her mind tried to place the information in the right context.

'Eh?' she said.

Cat smiled, and waited patiently for her to catch up.

'Wow,' Anna managed at length. 'Fuck. That's –'. And then she gave up, stood up and went round the table to give Cat a tight, long squeeze from behind.

'There were no bent knees or rings or any of that crap,' Cat said pre-emptively, once Anna was back in her chair, still slightly dazed and beaming at her like an idiot. 'I haven't turned into someone else. It just sort of came up, and we decided to do it.'

'When?'

'Sometime in spring? We haven't really worked out any details yet. But it's gonna be small and casual. You'll barely even know it's a wedding. More like a party where I happen to wear a white dress.'

'And Dylan a tuxedo?'

'Fuck yeah! Have you seen him in a tuxedo? He looks fucking hot!'

'You're gonna be Mrs Owens!' Anna teased, half-excited and half-terrified at the prospect.

'I will not!' Cat said sharply. 'I'm not changing my name. Like I said: I'm not turning into someone else.'

Anna smirked. 'You did say that. But you'll still be someone's wife!'

'Shut up!' But as much as she protested, Cat couldn't help but smile: she was going to be *Dylan's* wife. And no matter what else might be going on in her head, it was clear to Anna that this idea didn't scare her at all.

They talked no more about it that evening: they had neither the vocabulary nor the material to take this conversation any further. They had never fantasised about proposals and ceremonies and dresses, never imagined themselves as brides, and once they'd run through the facts they had nothing left to say, and happily moved on to other topics.

But they did talk about it again, a couple of months later, over coffee this time. The wedding had, of course, come up several times in the intervening months, as Cat and Dylan navigated the minefield of planning and came to Anna with random ideas, mostly concerning the music they'd play on the night. But this was premeditated, and arranged by Cat with a certain amount of gravity.

'I need to talk to you,' she said, and if she sounded a little nervous, Anna had thought nothing of it at the time.

They met in a café close to Anna's flat, one of those unbearably cool places with mismatched armchairs and battered sofas and rugs and amateur art for sale on the walls and board games strewn on every surface, but it was warm and cosy and did good coffee. They found a table and ordered cappuccinos.

'Weddings,' Cat said, to introduce the theme of the meeting, once their coffee had arrived. 'Two things. First, we're doing it in church.' She paused, and glanced at Anna anxiously. The question of a church wedding had been an ongoing debate, which had started from a resolute *no way*, travelled through various shades of *maybe* and had now, apparently, reached a tentative *yes*. 'Family politics,' Cat said darkly. 'Also, aesthetic reasons. Church prettier than town hall, etc.'

'So you're OK with it? You don't mind?'

Cat shrugged. 'I just want to marry him. I don't care how or where.' She smiled. 'Anyway, the point is: will you be my maid of honour? My *koumbara*?' She fiddled with a

Monopoly piece that happened to be on their table – a hotel – and spoke quickly. 'Because I really want you to. Dylan and I both want you to. But I know you don't like churches and all that...'

'Cat, stop! Of course I'll be your *koumbara*!'

'You will?'

'I will! If you're brave enough to get married in church, then I'm sure I can be brave enough to stand next to you while you do it.'

Cat lowered her gaze to her cup. 'I don't think I could do it without you,' she mumbled, before raising her head to look at Anna again.

They both stood up then, in almost perfect synchronicity, and met over the table in a hug, and wiped their eyes surreptitiously as they pulled apart and lowered themselves politely back into their armchairs. They exchanged a shy smile.

'Thank you,' Anna said.

'Thank *you*,' Cat replied.

Both their voices sounded strange, and Anna laughed.

'We're such awkward fucking people!'

'We are, aren't we?' Cat reflected. 'I never knew. Shall we start behaving normally again now?'

'Let's,' Anna agreed. She offered Cat a celebratory cigarette, which she accepted, though she'd ostensibly given up, and they smoked in companionable silence, stirring the froth in their coffees between sips.

'And the second thing?' Anna ventured a little later.

'What?'

'You said there were two things,' Anna reminded her, with a sense of foreboding; she couldn't believe Cat had forgotten what she'd summoned her here to talk about, which could only mean she was putting it off.

'Oh, yes. The second thing.' Cat crossed her legs, leaned forward, cleared her throat. 'Jack.'

'Jack.' And the usual loss of breath, always, when his name came up, that Anna would never get used to. 'What about him?'

'I want to invite him. But I understand – I mean – It's up to you...'

The room shifted. Not spun, exactly, but moved in a very disconcerting way. Anna gripped the armrests of her chair and then caught herself at it and arranged her hands carefully on her lap.

'No,' she said finally. 'It's not up to me. If you want him at your wedding, you should invite him.' She was surprised by how even her voice came out.

'I just thought... him and Toby. It would be nice. And Chris, but I don't think they'll come, not with the baby. But if you can't –'

'It's fine,' Anna cut in. 'It's your wedding. Invite him.'

'But it's not, though, is it? It's not fine.'

'No.' Anna smiled bitterly. 'But I'll get through it. I'll have to see him at some point anyway. And it's been, what –?' she paused, as if working it out, though she knew exactly how long – 'four and a half years! It's pathetic.'

'I never said –'

'I know you didn't. I'm sorry. But *I'm* saying it.' She took a deep, shuddery breath and felt it reverberate through her whole body. 'Invite him. I'll be fine.'

Cat looked completely unconvinced, and Anna hated that her personal history was casting a shadow on her wedding, when it should all be sunshine and happiness. She put on her bravest smile.

'In any case,' she said, as flippantly as she could manage, 'I'll be too busy with my official duties as your *koumbara* to pay much attention to Jack.' Her voice was too high, too bright, but they both pretended not to notice.

'OK,' Cat said, defeated, but also – Anna hoped – relieved. 'But if you change your mind.'

'I won't.'

'He might not come.'

'He will.' This much she knew: if Cat asked him, he would come. Jack would be there. *Jack would be there.* But as those words crystallised in her mind, took on the substance not of possibility, vague and distant, but of solid, unavoidable fact, it wasn't the thought of seeing him that sent a jolt through her this time. It was the thought that came straight after; bold, uninvited, and completely at home: she wanted to. Whatever it might do to her, she wanted to see him.

'Will you tell Robert?'

Anna shook her head. 'There's nothing to tell.'

It was the first time, she realised, that she had openly lied to Cat.

*

The hardest thing I ever did was walk away from Jack. This is the second hardest: to see him again. I've had months to prepare – Cat told me in January, and it's now April – but nothing could have prepared me for how it actually feels. It's not what I expected.

The first time is as bad as I thought. Worse. Devastating. It throws me so far and so hard that I see not other option but to run away. Which, given my history, is not surprising. It's what I do. There is plenty of precedent.

There are drinks the night before the wedding, in a bar that Cat likes in Kolonaki. The Sports Bar came up as a possible venue, but the guests from England and Wales, who are the main reason for out get-together this evening, have spent enough time in pubs; they want an authentic Greek experience out of their trip to Athens.

This place is exactly right. There is a small indoors space containing the bar and a few tables, unoccupied, because everyone's outside, in the back, where tired-looking citrus trees, like the ones that line most of the streets in Athens, are dressed in tiny white fairy lights, making this ordinary courtyard look like a magical, secret garden, despite being squeezed in between the grey high-rise buildings of the city centre. There are about a dozen tables, each topped with a tea light flickering in a glass jar, and our friends are gathered around them, holding cocktail glasses and bottles of beer and lit-up cigarettes drawing their gestures in the air like fireflies.

Robert and I get there early, a little past eight, minutes after Dylan and Cat, who've brought along Dylan's older brother, Rhys, who is to be his best man, and their cousin Pete. The parents, both sides, are having dinner together in a restaurant frequented by Cat's mum and dad and have been banned from attending: it's friends only tonight. More overseas visitors arrive, a steady trickle throughout the evening, depending on flight times and the distance of their hotels from the bar. Our Greek friends, culturally conditioned to show disdain for punctuality, turn up almost en masse, loud and unapologetic, just before eleven. Most of them still live in the northern suburbs, where Cat and I grew up, and they have made the long journey into town in shared cars and cabs. Robert hangs around with me for a while, but the pull of the British crowd is too strong to resist, and he soon drifts off to join them. I catch sight of him, every now and again, shaking hands with Dylan's friends from Cardiff, slapping Dylan vigorously on the back, clinking bottles with Rhys and, at some point, in a huddle with two guys I haven't been introduced to yet. He seems happy so I leave him to it, and keep myself in orbit around Cat.

I have been poised for Jack's arrival for hours, trying to hold myself together as I hyperventilate mildly through every conversation I have, and I'm completely blindsided when Lex shows up instead. I literally don't see her coming. She launches herself at me from behind, practically climbing on top of me, and I cry out in shock and then in excitement. We hold onto each other and jump around in circles like children, causing a few people to look up in alarm, before they realise what's happening and turn away, shaking their heads in amusement. I can't believe she's here. I knew she and Toby have been seeing each other since our leaving party, but neither of them had told me she was coming to the wedding.

'We wanted to surprise you!' Lex screeches, and I admit that they succeeded, noting the *we* and the easy way she says it and thinking, perhaps Sylvia finally got her wish.

'Where's Toby, anyway?'

'On his way. Having a shower, doing his hair, I don't know. I couldn't wait! But Anna –'

'What? Oh, sorry.' I cut her short, because Rhys is tapping me on the shoulder, wanting to know what's expected of him tomorrow, during the ceremony; Dylan, apparently, sent him over to ask. 'Sorry, Lex,' I say. 'I'll catch up with you in a bit.'

She looks uneasy, as if she's about to protest, but then she nods. 'Sure. I'll just go get a drink.'

I talk a very nervous-looking Rhys through the ceremony and his part in it (he will be in charge of the rings, while I'll be on wreath-swapping duty, which is fiddlier and more likely to go wrong), and then we head over to the bar to celebrate our newly forged bond with a shot. He is soon accosted by a gaggle of overexcited men, and I sneak away to look for Lex.

I find her at the back of the courtyard, talking to George, and I go up to her and slip my arm through hers.

'So you've met my brother.'

'Yeah!' Lex beams. 'Can you believe it? First person I spoke to!'

George smiles and gives Lex a sideways glance.

'Don't even think about it! She's taken.'

Lex snorts, while George does his best to look offended. 'Unbelievable,' he mumbles. 'My own sister.'

Lex tuts theatrically and George laughs, and it crosses my mind that if I were to set up him with any of my friends, it would be Lex, and how there is maybe more than one person in the world for each of us. For some of us.

'How's it going with Toby, anyway? This is pretty big, coming to the wedding together.'

'Yeah.' She smiles sheepishly, and her face sort of glows.

'Girl talk,' George interjects. 'Time to go. Great to meet you, Lex.' He gives her a sleazy wink, sticks his tongue out at me, and departs.

'It's going well,' Lex continues, dreamily. 'It's different, recently. Like we're a proper couple, you know? Has he said anything to you?'

'Not a lot. But Toby's a poker player.'

'What?'

'Cards close to his chest.'

Lex nods. 'I've noticed! But we've been spending a lot of time with his friends.' She pauses, gives me an uncertain look. 'Your friends? Though I have to say, that Sylvia's a bit intense.'

I laugh, and I'm about to ask if the tunnel has come up yet, when Lex reaches over and takes hold of my hand.

'Anna,' she whispers urgently, and in that same instant something changes in the quality of the air. I swivel around, in slow motion, hairs standing on end, and I see him, and the sight of him takes everything out of me, everything I consist of, and whips it up and swirls it around and flings it back in carelessly, haphazardly, and I can't move a single part of my body because it's all put together wrong. All normal functions shut down. Sound drains away, except for a dull throbbing around my temples, motion is suspended, and everything shimmers strangely. The word *swoon* pops into my head, unbidden, and then tumbles away, along with all my other words.

Jack is here. In this city, in this garden, a few metres away. Jack is standing outside the bar with Dylan and Cat. My gaze locks onto him and I can't break the link. I watch him as he and Dylan pat each other amicably and as he wraps his arms around Cat and lifts her off the ground. I watch him shift his weight from foot to foot – he does that when he's nervous, or excited – and throw his head back as he laughs. I watch him like prey watches a predator approaching: completely still, playing dead, but my eyes stay on him all the time. I don't blink. I'm not sure I'm breathing.

'Anna!' Lex is saying. 'Give me your glass!' I hear the panic in her voice and realise I'm gripping it so hard that it's about to shatter, but I cannot seem to let go. Lex prises my fingers off it, and puts it down on a table with a sigh of relief.

'He's gone to the bar,' she tells me and I nod, very slowly, because I've seen. Somehow I find myself sitting down, and I blink my eyes, at last, and focus on Lex.

'I tried to tell you earlier,' she says apologetically, as she hands me my drink. I drain it. 'We flew together. We're in the same hotel.'

'How did you know?' As close as Lex and I had become when we worked together, I never told her about Jack. It was part of my survival strategy, to have one place where nobody knew and nobody asked.

'Toby,' she says. 'He told me a few things. But I didn't realise how much... I thought you'd...'

'Moved on?'

She shrugs. 'Why didn't you tell me?'

'I wanted to forget.' But as I hear myself say it, I know it's a lie: I don't think I ever even tried.

'Doesn't look like it's worked. Fuck. I thought you were gonna pass out!'

This reaction is so normal that it snaps me out of my daze for a moment. I attempt a smile to convey how grateful I am for her support, for sensing it was needed despite not being told, but I don't think I've achieved the intended expression because Lex just looks alarmed. I give up.

'I have to go,' I tell her instead. 'Will you help me?'

'How?'

'Get him out of the way, so I can leave. I'm sorry. I just. I can't do this tonight.' My voice tilts into hysteria; I must sound completely deranged.

'You don't need to explain.' Lex has gone businesslike. 'I'm on it. Stay here.' She gives me a quick, firm hug and she's off, snaking her way through the tables to reach Jack at the other end. He's been joined by Toby and they both have drinks, and Lex points to an empty table midway down the garden by the side wall and draws them away. This is my cue.

I start to move and there's a second when my body veers to the right, of its own accord, and all I want to do is run to him and throw myself into his arms and put a stop to this, all of it, whatever it is, because it makes absolutely no sense. I fight it, stumble, correct my course and march, head down, straight to the exit.

I make two calls on my way home. One to Cat, to apologise and explain, and one to Robert, to lie. I don't feel bad. He hadn't even noticed I was gone.

***

It's Robert who's ill the next morning, but I have to keep up the pretence. I copy his symptoms, but I don't have to try too hard: I look like a ghost.

'How are you feeling?' he croaks.

'Better. A little nauseous. I don't know what came over me last night. It was probably the shots.'

'The shots,' Robert repeats, and groans. 'I know about the shots.'

'Sorry to abandon you.'

'S' alright. As long as you're OK.'

I bring him water, ibuprofen and coffee in bed, but it's neither out of love nor guilt: I'd do this for anyone.

But I know I have to tell him before the wedding. Before I see Jack again. I thought I was prepared but last night proved me wrong, and I cannot afford a confrontation with Robert this evening, if he finds himself standing next to Jack, unwarned. I don't want them standing next to each other at all: Robert and I have found some sort of equilibrium in the last few months, but I have seen how quickly scales can tip, and this is heavy stuff I'm dealing with.

I wait until he's up and about and halfway to coherence and drop it, casually, in the space between us. I actually manage to sound breezy. 'Oh,' I say, 'by the way, Jack's coming tonight.' I congratulate myself on the phrasing: tonight. As if last night never happened.

'Jack? As in your ex boyfriend?'

'Mmm,' I say distractedly, like I've already forgotten what we were talking about.

Robert does one of his pouts and his eyes narrow, while I carefully avoid making eye contact. 'Right,' he says curtly. 'Great.'

I act as though I haven't heard and disappear into the shower. I take as long as I can in there, but there is still something spiky about Robert when I come out, which, combined with his hangover, makes for a very volatile situation. But I have walked these eggshells before, and I know where to put my feet. I distract him with endless chatter about the wedding, drawing him in, unwilling though he is. I fuss over our outfits, ironing imaginary creases out of skirts and collars. I make jokes about how I'm useless in heels, and likely to fall over in the middle of the ceremony. He doesn't laugh but he gradually softens and by the time I leave, earlier, so I can spend some time with Cat before the wedding, the storm clouds have dwindled down to harmless wisps, drifting languidly across the horizon. There is real tenderness in the kiss he gives me at the door. I reciprocate with a long hug. Not guilt, but sadness.

The second time is as bad as the first. We're in the church courtyard, waiting to go in. There are close to a hundred people out here, but I sense him on the edge of the crowd as soon as he arrives: the nauseating tingling that alerts me to his presence; a feeling of being underwater; the cold shock that numbs my limbs. But this is not the time: the wedding is about to start. I make my way to the front of the church, past the friends and family filing in to take their seats, to where the priest is waiting with Dylan and Rhys. I am exposed here, but out of bounds, like the altar I stand before. This is my grace period: while I do my part in bringing Dylan and Cat together as husband and wife, I am untouchable.

I don't see Jack come in, and I'm glad that I don't know which part of the church he's chosen to sit in; it would be hard to keep my eyes away if I did. And then Cat arrives, and I take my place beside her as all four of us turn to face the priest, and there's a sanctity in this moment that has nothing to do with churches and gods and scriptures, and all other thoughts fall silent and still, just like the guests gathered solemnly behind me. I am here for Cat and Dylan; all of us are.

But at the end of the ceremony, after the rings have been exchanged and the wedding wreaths placed on the newlyweds' heads, tied together with a length of ribbon to symbolise their union, comes the dance of Isaiah. We line up, Cat and Dylan holding hands and Rhys and I behind them holding the ribbon up, as the priest, chanting the

hymns, leads us around the centre table three times. And as we turn and face the guests, my eyes meet Jack's.
 It's not what I expected, but it's what I knew. What I know, from before. Stillness. Like autumn leaves that have settled on the ground on a windless day. Like all the restless things have found where they belong and stopped searching; like all the pieces of the world have clicked into place and nothing needs to move. We move in circles, in a cloud of incense, in this celebratory dance, but it's stillness. Our eyes meet at every turn, three times, and it isn't pain like I expected. It is relief.

***

Cat has kept her word and the reception is a party where all of us happen to be very well dressed. Mostly: I have brought a pair of All Stars along, with Cat's permission, and I change into them as soon as we get to the venue. It's the garden of an old neoclassical house in the northern suburbs, converted to host parties and events; there is a paved area close to the house with tables and chairs for dinner, and decking, amidst plane trees, makes up the dance floor. There is no seating plan except for the older generations, and we all mill about happily, from table to table, toasting Cat and Dylan with cocktails from the open bar.
 Robert has barely left my side since we got here. I understand: Cat, Dylan, Rhys and I are still under the spell of the ritual we performed and he feels left out, and the prospect of coming face-to-face with my ex-boyfriend can't help – but I'm still irritated. The way he touches me is an assertion of ownership and his entitlement to be here, important in his own right, not as the boyfriend of the bride's best friend. He overstates his closeness to Dylan and Cat, and the hand he keeps on the small of my back as he shepherds me around feels like a violation.
 I realise he's been looking for Jack the moment he finds him.

'Is that him?' he asks. 'Is that Jack?' I look to where he's pointing and confirm that yes, that's Jack. I keep my voice flat and disinterested. Next thing I know, Robert stalks off in his direction, alpha dog protecting his territory, and I have no choice but to follow. He cannot know the mistake he's making or he would turn right around and go find someone else to talk to. He would place himself next to anyone but Jack. He doesn't know: he is no alpha dog here; he is a bad tempered puppy yapping at a pack of wolves.

Jack is standing with Toby and Lex; Robert struts straight up to him and thrusts his hand out.

'Jack,' he barks. 'I'm Robert. Anna's partner.' I cringe at the unearned familiarity and the pretension – *partner?* – but Jack is not fazed.

'Of course,' he replies pleasantly, as if he's been expecting him. 'Hi Robert.'

'Yeah,' says Robert, retracting the shaken hand and grasping for mine. I pull away and take a step back, just out of reach. For a second Robert's hand lingers, midair, before he recovers and slips it into his trouser pocket, in a gesture meant to exude casual confidence. 'How're you doing, man?'

Robert has never, to my knowledge, used the word "man" in this context before. But here is a black man, and he must be addressed as such.

I want to laugh. No: I want to punch Robert in the face, and then laugh. Jack, to his credit and my disappointment, does neither.

'Good,' he says. 'Thanks.' He keeps his expression neutral, but I'm watching him, and I see amusement – and something else, some uneasiness I can't quite decipher – flit across his features. Our eyes meet again, over Robert's shoulder, and he gives me a nod, which I return. We still haven't said a word to each other.

'And how are you finding Athens?' Robert persists. He now sounds like the official representative of the Greek Tourism Board.

'I love it,' Jack replies. 'It's good to be back.' I'm almost certain he means this neither as a deliberate dig at Robert nor a reference to our past, but it knocks the air out of Robert's puffed up chest. Does he know his mistake now? If he did, he'd walk away. But Robert doesn't move. He stands there, both hands in his pockets like a cowboy fondling his guns, staring up at Jack as he tries to stare him down, while Jack still smiles amicably and sways, gently, from foot to foot. I can't watch this anymore. I turn around sharply, to Toby and Lex, who are entirely entranced by the scene, and practically drag them off to the bar.

'Fuck,' I say, when we get there.

'Innit,' Toby concurs, the excitement tipping him, momentarily, back into South London.

Lex giggles nervously. 'Are you just gonna leave him there?'

I'm about to point out that Jack can look after himself when I realise that, of course, she means Robert. 'He can walk away any time he wants,' I say brusquely.

We order strawberry daiquiris – even Toby – and talk of other things.

When Robert joins us, some time later, he's got his pout back on, but I am done treading carefully when he's just gone trampling all over those tender little shoots that I've been trying to grow into a future for the two of us.

'So that's Jack,' he states.

This doesn't warrant a response and I give none.

'So you brought him to Athens,' he continues. The pout contracts into a grotesque pucker that would look funny if it weren't so vicious. 'And you didn't think to mention that.'

'I didn't think I had to,' I reply curtly. 'We were together for a long time. What did you expect?'

'I expected you to be my girlfriend,' he hisses. 'And not to show me up in front of that arrogant arsehole.'

And of all the mistakes he's made, this is the one we'll never recover from. Insulting Jack; playing himself against him. He doesn't know what he's doing. He doesn't know what he's just done. If I had any sense, I would end this thing right here, because Robert's just shown me exactly where my loyalty lies. But I don't.

I cast Lex and Toby an apologetic look and pull Robert aside. I am beyond anger; a strange calm comes over me, and I sound completely rational.

'What's this about? Are you jealous?'

'You pulled your hand away.'

'I know,' I say, 'I'm sorry. But you and I have each other. Jack's on his own. Do you really need to rub it in?'

Robert stares at me, wide-eyed. 'Are you actually asking me to spare your ex-boyfriend's feelings?' he says incredulously.

'I am asking you to be the bigger man. Can you do that? Just for this evening? Can you have the good grace to try?'

I am shocked by how conniving I can be. Robert loves the moral high ground, and I have just handed it to him. He cannot resist.

'OK,' he agrees grudgingly. 'I can do that. I can try.'

'Thank you,' I say and now, finally, I take his hand. Even my smile is an act. I don't feel guilty. Just for this evening, until this evening ends, I have cut myself loose. I give Robert a kiss on the cheek, and go off to find Cat.

After dinner we all drift over to the dance floor where George, DJ for the night, is doing his best to cater to everyone's requests while keeping his artistic integrity intact, but this is a wedding and it's proving very challenging. Robert is performing his bigger man duties with zeal and stays mostly away, happy in the company of his new Welsh friends, but he watches me, and I watch Jack. I don't need to: I am completely attuned to his movements. Even as I dance with Dylan and Rhys, join the Greek gang for a round of shots, share a clandestine cigarette with Cat and perform ill-advised downward dogs with Lex, I know exactly where he is. I don't go to him. I bide my time and spend it with other people, until much later, when the parents have left and the tables have been cleared and everyone's a little bit drunk, and I find myself, spellbound, gravitating towards him.

He is standing back from the dance floor, alone in the shadows, with his feet slightly apart and his arms crossed

over his chest, watching fifty sweaty people do the *Macarena*. I slip next to him and mirror his stance. He doesn't turn his head but, with a tiny shift sideways, he bumps me with his hip and I bump him back.
    'Hey,' he says.
    'Hey,' I reply.
    This is all we say. We say nothing else; we do nothing. We only stand together, side by side, leaning into each other lightly, as the *Macarena* becomes Bon Jovi becomes *Mr Jones* and time passes elsewhere, for other people, who dance and drink and talk and laugh as the world hurtles towards morning, while we stay still. And it never occurs to me how this looks or how I might explain it to Robert later, once we've pulled apart. There is no later. There is no Robert. There is nothing but the places where Jack's body touches mine, this seam that connects us: there is no pulling apart. But when it happens, when we do it – I don't know when or how – that's when we look at each other. We turn around and face each other and look. Time passes, elsewhere. And then, eventually, we turn away and walk in opposite directions.

The evening ends but the spell holds. I have cut myself loose but the seam holds. That spell: it wasn't cast tonight; that seam is stronger than it looks. There is no breaking it. There is no pulling it apart.
    The evening ends and it is Robert who has cut me loose but I follow him home, anyway, and he doesn't know what he's done. I follow him home and put the truth to sleep in our double bed, between us.

Nine

There are certain things that time cannot touch. Very few. Metal it turns to rust and bones to dust and the souls of those we've loved into ghosts and memories. Ancient temples fall to ruin and gods fall from grace, and people fall out of love and forget. Very few things can withstand the passage of time, its ruthless continuity, always moving on, always leaving moments behind, but in Anna's short lifetime there was one thing that did. Not the love. Love is a living thing and it evolves and expands and contracts and changes its shape and adapts to circumstances. And the love she had for Jack endured, but it knew to disguise itself, undiminished but not unaffected; it knew to flatten itself out to fit the space it was allocated. But the thing that brought the love into existence in the first place, the thing that opened the gate into this world to let it in, that thing – whatever it was – remained untouched.

After the wedding, Anna threw herself into her life with Robert with more vigour than ever before. She threw herself into it almost blindly, like a blinkered horse spooked by a loud noise behind it, trotting straight ahead, with a manic energy that whizzed and buzzed and drowned out all thoughts of that evening.

It had been the best time to see Jack again: when she and Robert were doing well, when, after months of clawing their way up to a reasonable standard of living, they had finally reached a nice, comfortable plateau, when they could both glimpse, if they looked ahead, a bright, clean horizon: not a breathtaking view, but a pleasant one, a view you could stroll towards, hand in hand, quite contentedly, if you didn't pay too much attention to the sights you passed along the way and all that you left behind. It had been the worst time, because there were no excuses, no rough patch to justify how easily she fell, how easily she would give this perfectly decent life up without a moment's hesitation, for a moment with Jack. And how a few moments stillness with Jack had annihilated two and a half years of moving ahead with Robert, wiped it out like it had been nothing more than a passing fancy, a lapse in the proper order of things.

Robert hadn't asked for an explanation. He hadn't brought up that evening at all. Perhaps some survival instinct had kicked in – too late – warning him that nothing good could come of it. Perhaps he really was trying to be the bigger man. There was no question of whether he had seen them; they had been hard to miss, completely conspicuous in the shimmering bubble they'd erected around themselves for privacy. Cat and Dylan, Lex, Toby, George and even some of her Greek friends had all mentioned it, in turn: the strange sight of Anna and Jack standing still in the half light as everyone danced.

'That looked a bit intense,' Dylan commented on the night, while Cat smoothed down her wedding dress awkwardly, conscious of her role in bringing this meeting about, and hugged Anna tightly, promising a dedicated session to discuss the incident.

'It was like you were in a separate world, completely cut off,' Lex had mused insightfully. 'It made me want to cry.'

'You did cry,' Toby corrected.

'I cried a little bit,' Lex admitted, glancing over at Toby, who shook his head at Anna in exasperation.

'Mate,' he said. 'You two need to sort yourselves out.' And with a smirk he added: 'Your boyfriend can't have been impressed.'

But Robert hadn't said a word. And Anna discovered, as the days went by and no confrontation came, that she was disappointed. That she'd been hoping for a confrontation to take the decision out of her hands. Had he asked her, she would have told him. She had played the scene out in her mind: how she would lower her head – not shame but regret – and say *I'm sorry, I cannot fight this. I tried, but I can't.* And Robert would understand and they would part amicably, blamelessly, powerless against the thing that had chosen Anna and Jack for itself, branded them with its mark so they could never belong to any other. *For some of us,* Anna would say, *there is only one person.* And she would set Robert free, to find a person of his own.

But this required courage, and neither of them had it. Neither of them was ready, yet, to initiative the closing sequence to their relationship. So Robert didn't ask and Anna didn't tell. Time passed.

While Cat and Dylan postponed their honeymoon until they could afford to do it how they imagined, Anna and Robert had one of their own. In the weeks after the wedding, Robert was considerate, a little careful with her, solicitous. He took an interest in her day, asked questions about her work, and made a point of telling her she was beautiful. One time, after an early shift at the bar, he came home with flowers, a slightly wilted bunch of red roses that made Anna feel vaguely sad, and turned brown at the edges the day after. He planned his nights off in advance so the two of them could go out for dinner or a movie; he called these evenings "dates". He turned talkative in bed – not the dirty talk of their early days but inquisitive, almost clinical – pausing mid-action to ask whether this particular type of thrust was working and how it could be improved, which led to some equally clinical orgasms, technically perfect but devoid of substance, somehow, like smiles that look good on the lips but don't reach your eyes.

Anna, in turn, turned to tricks and techniques for successful relationships prescribed by long-forgotten self-help books that she kept on the bottom shelf of her bookcase. She acknowledged the things he did for her and showed appreciation in the appropriate ways; she never failed to praise or reward him for his efforts, never criticised him if he failed. She stopped by to see him at work several times a week, listened to his rants about how the world was out to screw him over, again, with patience and sympathy, and often had dinner waiting for him when he came home. Her touch was gentle, her smile warm, her words inoffensive; her personality fenced in tighter than was strictly comfortable and chaffing a little where it rubbed up against Robert's, but peace was a powerful balm. If she went against her nature, daily, in many small ways, she told herself it was for a good cause. She understood that this was a performance: they were playing a couple, hunter and gatherer, strong and gallant man to devoted woman, obliging and obliged. As long as they kept within these archetypal roles, as long as neither of them strayed too far outside their boundaries they were safe, and their horizon stayed in view, a little foggier, perhaps, than it had been, but still there, still something to trudge towards, indefinitely.

It was those dinners that were her downfall. She had unwittingly set a precedent that she failed to observe, and the game was up. It was a June evening, a Tuesday, a little after nine. Anna had worked the morning shift at the studio and then taught three lessons back to back, and was still at her desk scribbling ideas for tomorrow's students when Robert came home. He walked in and dropped his bag on the floor with a thump.

'Hi,' Anna said, looking up briefly before returning to her notes.

Robert hovered by her desk. 'Is there anything to eat?' he asked.

'Nope.'

'You haven't cooked?'

'Nope. Only just finished my last lesson.'

Robert exhaled loudly through his teeth. 'So let me get this straight: I'm at work all day, slaving away behind the bar, while you lounge about here, and it doesn't even occur to you I might need some food when I get home.'

'Ha! I know, it's a disgrace!' Anna laughed, but Robert's expression was stony. 'Hang on. You're serious?'

'Course I'm bloody serious. I'm exhausted and I'm starving.'

'And I'm working!'

Robert snorted. 'Yeah. I can see. It looks hard.'

Anna couldn't quite believe this was happening. The last few weeks had taken the edge off her caution, and she'd forgotten how to navigate Robert's inexplicable mood switches, his sudden, unearned cruelties. 'Please tell me you're joking right now,' she said weakly.

'Does this sound like a joke to you? That I come home at nine pm and have to make my own dinner? Is that funny to you?'

'It's funny that you think I should have done something about it.'

'You could have, if you had any consideration for me.'

'I was working!'

'You could have taken a break.'

'A break to rustle up a meal for you?' Robert frowned, as if he couldn't see a problem in this sentence. 'Do *you* take breaks from work to cook?'

'No!' he said with a nasty chuckle. 'I have a proper job.'

Anna did not grace this with a response. 'I started work at eight o'clock this morning and I'm still working,' she said instead. 'How about *you* cook for *me*?'

'Not my job.' Deadpan.

'But it is mine?'

Robert shrugged: *obviously*.

'Is it traditional roles you want? Cause I can do that. I can quit both my jobs and let you earn all the money like a real man while I stay at home, painting my nails and reading cook books, and preparing delicious meals for you for when you come home after your twelve-hour day. Do you want to do that?'

Sharp intake of breath and a heavy pause as Robert organised his rage into sentences, an army preparing to attack, but she cut him off.

'Because if not, then I suggest you go make yourself some cheese on toast and leave me alone.'

It was a rare occasion when Robert did what he was told, but this was one of them. Without the cheese on toast. He gave her a hateful look, so hard and cold that it actually sliced through her despite the armour of her anger, and stomped off to the bedroom, slamming the door behind him.

Anna stayed at her desk, scrawling the word FUCK several times all over her notes, and then, in small letters at the very bottom: *this has to end*. She stared at the words for a while, before tearing the page out of her notebook, scrunching it up into a ball and throwing it in the bin.

Never go to bed angry, the books said. But Anna didn't have it in her to attempt a reconciliation, when it wasn't the differences that were irreconcilable, but the people who owned them. She just didn't go to bed at all. She slept on the sofa, in her clothes.

The next morning Robert woke her up with a steaming cup of coffee that he placed next to her on the coffee table. He sat on the edge of the sofa by her feet and sipped his own coffee in silence. They were polite with each other, almost formal, but neither of them made a move to patch things up. The fabric of their intimacy was too worn out, too ragged to stitch together with apologies and promises; it wouldn't hold.

Still, she didn't give up. Like a poker player who knows she'll be knocked out in the next round, she kept going all in, holding out for the hand that would turn her luck around. Betting everything on a pair of twos and putting up parts of herself, as collateral, so she could stay on for another round. But the game was up: all the cards had been dealt, and there were no aces left in the pack. All they had was bad poker faces, reckless bluffs and a stack of plastic chips that it was too late to cash in and get themselves back.

Peacetime was over, and a tentative truce established in its place. Anna didn't cook and Robert learned to pick up takeaways on his way home. He stayed out later and later after work, and Anna rarely visited the bar: the sight of Robert performing his cheeky and cheerful barman routine had begun to make her stomach turn. She avoided being at home when he was around; she took long bus journeys across town, mostly northbound to Kifissia, visiting friends or, sometimes, just going there and coming back. The traffic of Athens, a curse to most, was a blessing, the slow, juddery journeys like meditation, stilling her restless thoughts as the bus moved through the city streets. Robert never asked where she'd been. Their conversation was stilted, forced, and any affection between them – open-eyed pecks of hello and goodbye that often, deliberately, missed the lips – so mechanical that it didn't deserve the name. The only time they still resembled a couple was on those few and far between occasions when they were out with other people. They would slip into their double act then and make their friends laugh but, unlike in the past, they were careless with their words and often took it too far, playful sarcasm quickly degenerating into undisguised spite. They had vicious, screaming arguments that flirted with violence – once, Anna pushed Robert, hard; another time he threw a bowl against the wall – that left them both raw and shaking with exhaustion. And the sex was not for making up, though it often succeeded these fights: no longer a union but a confrontation, it only took the battle to another arena – the bed, the sofa, the kitchen floor, any surface they could slam each other against – where they would crash into each other with a passion that was destructive, the physical expression of an anger that couldn't be mollified any other way. The cuts and bruises it left them with were not the kind you'd run your finger over, afterwards, with sweet longing.

But worse than all that were Robert's casual cruelties, under the belt blows delivered swiftly, out of nowhere, with the precision of a martial artist, when she was least prepared. There were moments like that, still, moments equally of weakness as of strength, when Anna would lower her defences and allow herself to believe there might still be something left to salvage, something left to mend. And that's when Robert would strike. He was no martial artist: these moves would be unethical, illegal in any noble discipline, but there was no nobility in this. It was a cold discipline, calculated to undermine. To make everything about her small, so he could stand next to her and have something to look down on. A very English thing: to cut her down to size.

There was an afternoon in July when she decided to surprise Robert at work. She had felt a stirring of something – love? hope? desperation? – and acted upon it, before she could change her mind. She called Cat and suggested they meet at the bar for coffee and when they got there, before Robert had spotted them, she lingered at the doorway for a moment and watched him. She tried to see him as she saw him once, the good, gentle side of him that they had both turned away from, and she walked towards that remembered man, scared but hopeful, cautiously ready to invite him in. She gave him a long, hard hug and she felt him respond, felt him shudder and surrender to it, and she though maybe he understood what she was offering, and that he might pick it up, tenderly, in his hands, like a bird fallen out of the nest, and warm it back to life.

She and Cat found a table close to the bar and were enjoying their iced coffees and the merciful air-conditioned coolness of the room, the relief it provided from the overheated streets of midsummer Athens, when Robert, with a tilt of his head, summoned her over to where he stood.

Anna approached him, smiling, and touched him gently on the arm. 'What's up?' she said.

'I need to tell you something,' Robert replied, gravely. There was something odd about his tone, didactic almost. 'Take a look around,' he urged. 'All the other girls in here are in skirts and dresses and they take care of themselves.' He paused, to let her take this in. 'And look at you.'

Anna did; she glanced down at her summer uniform of vest top, denim shorts, bare legs and neon green All Stars. She saw nothing unusual.

'What's wrong with me? This is how I've always dressed.'

'It's not feminine,' Robert said mournfully, as if this failing of Anna's was the cause of great pain to him. 'It's embarrassing,' he added, while gaping in open admiration at a skinny redhead in a crotch-skimming strapless dress who was just then tottering her way to the bar in open-toe wedges. 'I'm not saying you should change *completely*,' he continued, generously. 'But how about you make a bit of an effort?'

It took Anna a few seconds to recover her speech, but when she did her voice was steady, even, just loud enough for Robert to hear and drop the conciliatory smile from his face.

'How about you go fuck yourself?' As graciously as she could, she collected her shoulder bag and her tattered pride and a concerned-looking Cat and staggered out the door in her flat, embarrassing shoes.

'What the fuck just happened?' Cat asked as she ran to keep up with her.

But Anna just shook her head and carried on walking.

It was the worst time, but she didn't talk about it. She couldn't bring herself to say the words, the words that had been said and the words that hadn't and hung over her head like a guillotine on a frayed rope. *This has to end.* She couldn't bring herself to end it, and she was ashamed. At another time she might have sought her friends' advice, let them in to the truth that she was living with; she could have told them everything and let their firm, steady hands pick her up and stand her on her feet, her kind, lovely, loyal friends who would never judge her – but she judged herself. How could she stay with Robert, through all this, when she had been so quick to walk away from Jack? What kind of person did that make her, how small? She was ashamed and that shame bound her to Robert tighter than love ever had.

Cat had tried to talk to her, and so had Lex; Laura was always there, at the end of the phone. Dylan had broached the subject tactfully, George less so.

'How are things with Robert?' they wanted to know.

'Fine,' Anna replied. 'They're fine.'

Nobody mentioned Jack.

They went on holiday for a week in August. Cat's parents had a summer house in Paros, just outside Paroikia, the island's capital, that could sleep up to six. Cat and Dylan took one bedroom, Anna and Robert the other and Rhys was on the sofa bed in the living room – a double, convenient in the event he picked up one of the Greek ladies he had apparently developed a taste for during the wedding. When Lex and Toby made a spur of the moment decision to join them, Anna called Laura and asked her to come along, too; she had been promising to visit ever since Anna left London, and it had been too long.

'Can I bring Julian?' Laura asked, and Anna said the more the merrier and put her in touch with Lex so they could look into accommodation together. It turned out that Cat knew of a bungalow for rent a few minutes from the house, two double rooms and a kitchenette, and the owner was a long-time friend of her dad's so they got it for surprisingly cheap.

It was the best time: all of her closest friends, in one place, with hot sand between their toes and cold drinks in their hands and nothing to worry about except which dishes to order for lunch, but Anna had approached the holiday with almost as much trepidation as excitement. The comparisons she might be forced to draw made her nervous; she wasn't sure how her relationship would bear up against three happy couples in such close proximity. The newlyweds, still delighting in calling each other husband and wife, with more awe and less irony than they might have intended, for all the accompanying winks and smirks; the brand new lovers, discovering new delightful things about each other every day; and the unexpected success story that was Lex and Toby, who just seemed delighted with one another all the time. None of them were blatant about it; they were subtle, if anything, understated in their good fortune, but it shone off them, so bright that it made your eyes sting.

As Rhys succinctly put it on their first evening out, looking around the table with an expression of utter distaste: 'For fuck's sake! There's too much *happiness* around here.'

Don't worry, thought Anna bitterly as she sat stiff and stifled next to Robert, the resentment on this side of the table should balance it out.

But it didn't work out that way. Love, this time, did in fact conquer all and the concentrated force of it, helped along by Rhys' dark humour that, paradoxically, had a way of lightening any mood, seeped into the sealed off, dried up places where Anna and Robert festered, and got them moving again. By day three they both realised, to their mutual surprise, that they were no longer pretending to tolerate each other's company for the sake of appearances: there were moments when they actually enjoyed it. They could laugh together again, meet each other's eyes without hastily looking away, and when Robert, unthinkingly, rubbed sun lotion into Anna's shoulders, she didn't recoil from his touch. Looking back, Anna saw these – a smear of sun cream, reaching up to gently brush off a stray eyelash, a hand on a knee, an arm draped casually across the shoulders – as the last gestures of unforced affection between them.

It wasn't a fresh start, by any means. There were all out of fresh starts, but they were able, at least, to talk of one last try. They were able to talk, when all they had done for weeks was shout or attack each other with pointed silences.

One evening, drowsy and relaxed after a full day on the beach and a late, wine-infused dinner at home, they found themselves alone in the little courtyard outside their bedroom. Robert, leaning forward in his plastic chair, with his elbows resting on his knees and his head clasped between his hands, began the conversation with a sigh.

'It's been really bad, hasn't it,' he said flatly, the answer already given by the missing question mark. 'How did we let it get so bad?' He dropped his head down, arms now dangling between his legs.

'I never wanted it to be this way,' he went on. 'I never wanted to lose you.' His voice cracked and faded into the quiet of the night.

Anna left her chair and shuffled over to him, on her knees. She took his hands; he still didn't look up. And it was ironic that he squandered himself on being tough, on being hard and impenetrable, when it was now that he was helpless and soft that Anna loved him the most. She probably loved him more than she ever had before, but she loved him like someone she'd already left behind, that nostalgic, regretful love for things long lost, or given up, or destroyed.

She tightened her grip around his fingers; she had no other reassurances to give.

'Is it too late?' he asked. 'Can we give it one more try?'

'One last try,' Anna said, as Robert finally lifted his head and sought her eyes, the substitution instinctive but necessary: no more. This last try, but no more.

On their last day at the beach, as dusk fell and they all lingered, reluctant to peel themselves off the still-warm sand, Robert stood up, without explanation, and took himself off for a walk. He was gone for about ten minutes – Anna caught glimpses of him bending down, rummaging around in the sand – but he didn't sit back down on his towel when he returned. He stood by her feet, nudged her with his toe and said her name. He held out his hand. His expression, what Anna could make out in the fading light, was a mixture of eager and shy. She took his hand and he helped her up and walked her to a spot a few metres away.

'Look,' he said, pointing down.

There, in the wet sand, was a flower constructed of seaweed and pebbles and branches from the trees, its stem just brushing the line where the water swooped up and frothed and drew back with a gentle whoosh. 'For you.'

Anna knelt down and stroked its seaweed petals, gently, with the tip of her finger. She tried to commit it to memory, this beautiful ugly thing that Robert had made for her, but she found, as she prepared a place in her mind to store it, that it was already there. It was already a memento of a moment that had passed. She was experiencing this as a narrative, a story being told sometime in the future, long after Robert's frankenstein flower had been washed away, unresisting, by the gentlest of waves. She thought again of the absurdity of living your life in the third person, in the wrong tense. She thought again: no more. She wrapped her arms around Robert's legs and cried, for Robert, for herself, for everything they had tried to put together and that would scatter, like this flower, and drift out to sea.

'Oh god,' Robert said, crouching down to join her on the sand, 'is it that bad? Has my flower traumatised you?'

Anna smiled through her tears. 'It's the best thing you've ever given me,' she said.

It was in the bittersweet days that followed this encounter, the first few days of their one last try, that first person Anna stepped back into her life and sent that text message to Jack. She saw no contradiction in this, no betrayal, though she was aware that Robert wouldn't agree. But you can't betray someone who's never had your loyalty. You can't betray someone who's never had your heart. She had never promised either of these things to Robert; by the time she met him, they were no longer hers to give. Perhaps there was some duplicity in this, in not explicitly telling him she had neither heart nor loyalty to offer, that he'd have to make do without, but it had not been intentional. She had genuinely thought that they could make something together; she had honestly tried, crippled though she was, to make something new, something wholesome, something whole. And those parts of her that she *had* promised Robert, in good faith, the parts that she had put into this, to make it work – those parts had been faithful, would stay faithful to the end.

She hadn't betrayed Robert. It was the way she lived that felt, increasingly, like a betrayal. It was living with a man who didn't have her heart. It was herself she had betrayed

– not Robert, not even Jack – when she had made the choice to live this way. Sending that text message was the only pure, the most honest thing she had done in a long time. There was no guilt attached to it, no shame, and no expectations, either. It wasn't a call to action. It was a simple statement of fact, an acknowledgement of truth. She told no one, not Cat, not Laura, not Lex. It was a truth between her and Jack, not secret but private. She wanted nothing more from Jack, for now. She hoped for nothing. He knew, she knew, and that was enough.

Robert wouldn't agree. It would hurt him if he knew, and she could understand why. But you can't betray someone who's never given you his trust. And Robert hadn't, not ever, not fully: a man who knows he can't be trusted will never truly trust. But Jack had. And maybe that was the first betrayal, that: when she walked away. Not later, but then, right at the end, when all this began. When she broke the trust of a man who had given her everything but a reason to doubt him. When she had doubted him and taken his trust away, without a word of explanation. That.

*

It happens on the same day as Robert calls me a teacher. It is his parting gift to me before he leaves for work. He doesn't know, as he slams the door on his way out, that when he comes back tonight I will be completely out of his reach.

He's woken up in a foul mood. I can tell by the way he glares at me before he's even fully conscious. I slip out of bed, wash my face, brush my teeth and make my first cup of coffee, with the kitchen door shut so I don't disturb Robert and give him cause for a fight. He doesn't need to be up for another hour or so.

    I have a light day ahead: no yoga studio, and only the one Greek lesson in the early afternoon. I'm meeting Cat and Dylan for lunch afterwards – they're just back from their belated honeymoon – but otherwise the day is wide open. It's a perfect winter's morning, crisp and bright, the sun massive in the cloudless sky, a December sun that cuts through the cold and warms up your skin. I decide to dig out my rollerblades and go in search of adequate terrain. There's a spot close to George's flat frequented by skateboarders and breakdancers, with an actual, old-school boom box busting out scratchy tunes: a long stretch of grey marble tiles, seamless and smooth. It runs along the side of the Museum of Contemporary Art, but nobody seems to mind the kids and the boom box being there, as long as they stay away from the entrance and don't crash into the art lovers and the passers-by. I think I might join them. Perhaps they can even give me some tips on turning and stopping in my blades without falling over; I am completely out of practice and injury, to my ego if not my knees, is more than likely.

    But I can't find my rollerblades. I search in the two most likely places, our storage cupboard in the hallway, and the tall, narrow one in the kitchen, where we keep the mop and bucket and the hoover and random items that don't belong anywhere else, and I unearth some interesting artefacts, but there is no sign of my rollerblades. As a last resort, I decide to take a look in our wardrobe: there's a bit at the bottom, on Robert's side, where I vaguely remember shoving some stuff, months ago, when I ran out of storage space elsewhere. I creep into the bedroom and rummage around quietly, as quietly as possible; Robert stirs and I freeze, but he settles down again and I carry on. I pull out a plastic bag containing odd, orphaned socks, several pairs of Robert's shoes, an old Nokia charger, a crumpled up t-shirt and a tie that has slipped off the rail and there, right at the back, tied together by the laces, are my rollerblades. I lift them out and I'm about to start putting things back in when I see it, shiny white and out of place beneath a pair of mud-encrusted trainers: a bundle of papers, two hundred odd sheets of printed words. My manuscript.

I pick it up gingerly and hold it to my chest.

'Robert,' I say softly. Then louder: 'Robert!'

'What?'

I get up, cross to the bed and drop my book – its pages creased and curling, a smear of something dark on the title sheet – onto the bed next to his face.

'This.' My work, my only printed copy, my bravest thing, my token of trust given only to him, that he shoved in the bottom of our wardrobe, stashed away like a shameful secret.

He peels his eyes open and there's a flash of remorse as his gaze alights on the object before him, but the next instant it turns to scorn.

'Yeah?' he says defiantly. 'What about it?'

'It was under your shoes.'

He doesn't respond.

'Did you read it?'

A moment's hesitation, then: 'No.'

'Why not?' I cannot even begin to fathom this, how he could have it, hold it in his hands – his girlfriend's novel – and not read it, out of curiosity, if not pride. If not love.

A blink, a pursing of the lips, the smallest movement of the shoulders. 'I just didn't. What does it matter?'

'It matters because...' I'm grasping, desperate to believe this is a misunderstanding, that Robert, somehow, doesn't realise the significance of what I've given him, and the cost of not having read it. That it'll all be OK if only I explain. 'Do you know what this is to me? It's all I've got. If I'm a writer. Without that, I don't know who I am.'

'Well,' Robert says, sitting up abruptly, 'if that's your problem, I can help you. You're not a writer. You're a teacher. And you know what they say,' he can't resist adding: 'those you can't...'

And it's not just the words, but his evident pleasure in saying them, the sneer, the contempt. I don't know this man. I don't know either of us in this room. I don't know who this girl is, who carries on pleading.

'But...' I hear her stutter. 'I don't understand. Why are you being so cruel?'

The stranger-boyfriend snorts. 'Get over yourself, darling,' he says, taking his time to imbue every syllable with disdain. 'I'm only telling you the truth. And the sooner you accept it, the happier you'll be.'

He flings the sheets off and bounces out of the bed, his mood apparently lifted by the wisdom he's just imparted, scattering my manuscript all over the floor in the process. Robert steps over it, without a glance, and leaves the room.

I sit down on the bed he's just vacated and I don't move until he's left for work. I don't speak, not even when he comes back into the bedroom to get dressed, makes a great show of wading through the items I've taken out of the wardrobe to reach his clothes, and instructs me to tidy up when I'm done sulking. I have absolutely nothing to say.

I don't go rollerblading. I stay at home staring at walls. I get through my lesson, somehow, with apologies to Beth, who's the jolliest, most forgiving woman ever, and doesn't deserve a bad teacher.

'Don't be silly, love,' she says, with a motherly hand on my shoulder. 'You're grand.'

Her kindness brings me close to tears. 'Boyfriend trouble?' she guesses.

I nod weakly, embarrassed, and she gathers me into a big, squishy hug. She doesn't prod, for which I'm grateful. She doesn't try to give me advice.

'Go make yourself a cup of tea,' she tells me, simply. 'It'll pass. Everything does.'

It doesn't pass but it fades, and by the time I meet Cat and Dylan for lunch, I'm ready to hear all about their Scottish honeymoon. But they don't want to talk about that.

'We saw Jack,' Cat announces.

I lower my menu and shake my head. 'I don't want to know.' I'm surprised that I have to tell her, even more so that she doesn't back down.

'Actually,' she insists. 'I think you do.' Beside her, Dylan nods somberly.

Their itinerary, Cat explains, took them through London on the way back: they caught the train down from Edinburgh and spent two nights in town, catching up with friends.

'We met up with the old gang,' she says. 'Even Chris and Sylvia: they got a babysitter. And Jack...'

Jack was with a woman. This is what they want to tell me, what they think I need to hear. I go cold. I've always known it as a possibility, but I don't have the capacity to handle it as fact. I don't want to imagine him with someone else, looking at her, touching her. I imagine, instead, sticking my fingers in my ears and repeating nonsense words to block it out. I don't want to hear it.

But Cat is saying something else. 'He couldn't stop talking about you.'

'What?' I yell, only because this isn't what I was expecting, but it must sound like I'm accusing her of something, because Cat looks mildly panicked and tries to make excuses.

'It wasn't me, I swear! I didn't start it.'

'She didn't,' Dylan confirms.

'He barely even said hello to me. Just: *where's Anna? How's Anna? What's going on with Anna?*'

'What did you say?'

'I said you're fine. I said you're doing well.'
'And Robert?'
'Yeah,' Cat says, nodding. 'He asked about that too. But Anna...' – here she exchanges a glance with Dylan – 'he said he misses you. He said he loves you.'
'Loves me.'
'He told both of us,' Dylan supplies. 'Separately.'
'Loves me. In the present tense.'
Nods from both of them.
'In what context?'
'No context. *I miss her, you know. I love her.* Something like that.'
'Right,' I say, and I'm suddenly insanely, irrationally angry. 'And he thinks he should be telling you that *why*?' I slam my palms into the table, causing cutlery to rattle and my friends to lean back, not so discreetly. 'Cause he *knows* you'd tell me.'
'Yeah,' Cat agrees. 'Of course he knows. He obviously wants you to know.'
'Why? What's the fucking point?'
I try to roll a cigarette and notice my hands are shaking; loose tobacco goes flying everywhere, all over the tablecloth, my upside-down plate, my still-folded napkin. 'How the fuck dare he?' I mutter repeatedly, like a crazy person, while Cat and Dylan look on nervously. I eventually manage to construct a vague cigarette shape, and light it. I take a long, deep drag.
'What the fuck am I supposed to do with that?'
It is irrational. It is insane. Because I am the queen of out of context. Because I sent him a message from a bus, apropos of nothing at all, stating a destiny – and yet I am surprised by love. Because I am a hypocrite. Because I have a live-in boyfriend. Because I miss him too. But what am I supposed to do with love?
Neither of them has the answer; none of us speak. I smoke and shake my head and they watch me, motionless, until Cat picks up her menu and waves it over the table, as if she might fan my troubles away along with my cigarette smoke. 'How about we order some food?' she suggests.

But I feel queasy. 'I don't think I'll ever eat again,' I state dramatically, just as Dylan says 'Not yet.' They exchange another look, a short negotiation. 'There's something else,' he tells me. Cat sighs and puts her menu down on top of her plate, folds her hands over it, tilts her head sideways: *go ahead*. 'You know that wedding, Chris and Sylvia's wedding? When I first met Jack. He was talking about you then, too.'

'Is that why you were being so weird with me?'

'Well, yes, because... I didn't know you that well, then. You hadn't told me what happened. And he said...' He trails off, as if reconsidering starting along this path.

'He said what?'

'He said he didn't know why you left him.'

There is no metaphor to describe the impact of these words, but the silence afterwards is exactly like I imagine the aftermath of an explosion: thick, deadly, impossible to bear, almost more devastating than the blast itself, because the worst that could happen has happened, and there can be no going back.

'Like I said,' Dylan continues apologetically, 'I didn't know you that well, and you never talked about it. And I thought...'

'He thought you were some cold-hearted bitch,' Cat interjects drily. 'I put him straight.'

'Is that what Jack said? That I was a bitch?'

'No! Not at all. He only had good things to say about you. I think he actually called you "wonderful". But, I mean, the man looked completely heartbroken. I didn't know what to think. Anyway, Cat filled me in. And she said – we agreed – to leave it be.'

I remember it, that day after the wedding, the palpable tension between them; how Cat had intervened, more than once, to enforce Dylan's silence.

'I'm sorry,' she says now, taking over from Dylan. 'I don't know if it was the right thing. But you'd just met Robert and you seemed OK and you said you were happy. I didn't see what good it would do.'

He didn't know why.

'I'm sorry,' she says again, when I don't respond, lost as I am in the implications of this, the *what ifs* it raises. 'I was trying to protect you.'

She looks almost frightened and I reach, through my turmoil, to touch her hand. 'It's OK,' I tell her, because she needs me to. I'm not sure it's the truth.

I turn to Dylan. 'You weren't convinced.'

'Convinced?'

'By Cat's explanation. You still thought I might have been wrong to leave. You still suspected me to be a bitch.'

'Maybe a little bit,' Dylan admits, with a grin. 'But then I got to know you. And later, when I read your stories...' He doesn't need to elaborate. My stories are all alternative endings and the potential futures they might bring; the life we once had projected into imagined futures. They are endings that allow for futures to be had, the futures we would have had in stories whose endings don't amount to the end. They are not the stories of a cold-hearted bitch.

'And now? Why are you telling me now?'

'Now I think there's a chance.'

'That I'm a bitch? That I was wrong?'

'To make it right.'

Love. In the present tense.

'Excuse me,' I say, and leave the table.

Outside the restaurant, I pull my phone out of my jacket pocket and dial his number from memory. I'm operating on primal instincts and it's easier to reach inside and grasp for the digits than to try and figure out how my contact list works. My hands are still shaking and the keyboard tones sound absurdly loud.

He answers on the second ring.

'Anna?' His voice – surprised, inquisitive, a little excited – and I'm mesmerised. It isn't soothing, talking to Jack; it doesn't take away the anger, the confusion, the pain. It's like none of it ever existed. My reason for calling slips away, but I throw myself at it, wrestle it to the ground, shout it into the phone:

'What the fuck!'

'I'm sorry?'
'What the fuck are you doing?'
'What am I – I'm not doing anything. What's going on, baby? Talk to me.'
It's funny how it's another word when Jack says it. But he mustn't say it. He can't. He's not allowed.
'Don't call me that,' I snap, although something inside of me, the honest part, has just rolled over on the floor with its belly exposed, submitting to be stroked, or be killed. I have no defence against this man.
'OK,' he says. 'But tell me. What happened?'
'What happened! You! Saying things to my friends!'
'You mean Cat?'
'Yes Cat! And Dylan!'
'What did I say?'
'Are you fucking kidding me?'
'Not in the least,' he replies calmly, seriously. 'We spent a whole evening together. I said a lot of things.'
I get it now: he's not being evasive. He wants me to say it. He wants the words spoken between us, broken out of their second-hand narrative and perched on the crossed wires of this conversation, for both of us to hear.
I whisper it. 'That you miss me. That you love me?'
'OK.'
'Not OK! You can't just say these things to people! It's not fair. You can't. I can't.'
'You can't what? Anna – what do you want?'
And it slams me against a wall, this question. Because I want. I want the story rewritten. I want the futures we should have had. I want one of my alternative endings, any one of them, anything other than –
'How's Robert?'
- *this*. Anything but this. I want –
'Jack...'
'He seems like a good guy,' he says, and, oh god, I can hear how hard he's trying, how he's changing the truth to make it easier for me. But this, Jack putting himself in the path of pain so it doesn't reach me, hurts more that being hit by the oncoming train ever could. Shattered bones have

nothing on it, and mine are made of rubber. I have no idea what's holding me up.

Words. An attempt at sentences. 'He... Yes. But. I'm just trying... It's not like –'

'Anna,' he interrupts me, but so gently. 'Do what you've gotta do. Be happy. You should be happy.'

Shattered bones will heal and you might walk again, but I don't know how to come back from this. I don't know if there's anywhere to come back to. This sounds like Jack letting me go. The blast, the silence, the worst thing that could have happened: it wasn't the worst, after all. Because if Jack is letting me go, he has been holding onto me all these years. And what am I supposed to do with that?

I do nothing. I stand on impossible legs, quivering like a leaf destined to be blown away by the next gust, and listen to the rustle of Jack's breath and the thumping of my own heart, which insists on beating its tune. Impossibly, everything continues as before.

'You should be happy,' he repeats, as if it's some sort of spell, but it doesn't stick, and all I can say is 'I'll try.' It has a ring of truth to it, at least.

And silence.

And heartbeats.

And breathing. In and out.

And: 'Are you writing?'

I consider lying but of course this is Jack and I can't. 'No,' I admit.

'Baby,' he says, and I don't correct him this time, 'you've gotta write. No matter what else is going on. It's who you are.'

Of course. This is Jack.

'OK.'

'Promise me.'

'Promise you,' I say. I say 'Take care.'

I miss you too. I love you too: this is what I don't say before I end the call.

I go home, after thanks and apologies to Cat and Dylan, who seem desperate for me to stay and attempt to entice me with food, with drink, with company, with anything – but there is nothing that I want; I promise them another time and I go home. I go home, on foot, slowly, taking the longest route through Parliament Square and the National Gardens, where children feed caged goats and rabbits through the bars, and peacocks scream and fan their tail feathers and a mutant population of bright green parakeets twitters excitedly in the trees and red-faced joggers puff on, determined, and up the hill through Kolonaki, past the coffee drinkers and the smokers crowding the sunny side of the pavements and misting the air with their conversations. I go home, through the squeaky front door with the tarnished brass handle of better days, up the stairs and into my flat, and I have come full circle: I am not a writer. I am a writer. It's who I am.

I go home, and I do the only thing I can do: I start writing.

Ten

It was a few weeks before Anna told Robert. There was no sense of urgency, no immediate need for action. If anything, there was a faint hue of irrelevance, of inconsequentiality colouring everything she said or did or thought about, after her conversation with Jack. There was an air of anticlimax, of wandering aimlessly through the flatlands of a desolate landscape, razed by a passing disaster that had, nonetheless, passed: there was nothing, now, to be done. Nothing to do, except write.

So she wrote every day, before work, before bed, in between lessons, picking away at the last few chapters of her novel that had once seemed like an insurmountable obstacle, a solid wall that she couldn't break through, until, word by word, one by one, they began to take shape. With every sentence, every paragraph, every chapter she completed, she thought of Jack. Every full stop she placed: Jack. Letting her go was not the freedom she wanted, nothing she would have ever asked for, but he had set her words free when he reminded her of who she was. And he might never read these words, but he had put them on the page as much as Anna had; he had been there, reminding her, every time her fingers touched the keyboard.

Robert, those rare times she was aware of his presence, appeared almost see-through, less than a ghost. He did not haunt her, he did not rattle any chains; he drifted from work to home, from room to room, irrelevant, inconsequential, unworthy of exorcism. He did not give her chills or bring her messages from beyond; he gave her nothing, he brought her nothing, and there was nothing to be done. There was no sense of urgency until, suddenly, there was.

She was with George when Robert came home that evening. They had spent the day together, a Sunday; they'd had lunch with their parents in Kifissia, then caught the bus back into town and to Anna's flat, where they'd passed the afternoon with coffee, cigarettes and endless games of backgammon. Robert was on the lunchtime shift, the busy one, gloomy winter Sundays making every British expat in the city nostalgic for the comfort of something covered in gravy and the familiar scent of stale beer. He made it back around seven, to find Anna and George bent over the backgammon set on the coffee table, in the middle of a particularly suspenseful game, cigarettes burning away in the heaving ashtray. They both paused, Anna clutching the dice in her hand, about to throw, and looked up as Robert walked into the room.

'Hi,' he said, shrugging his coat off his shoulders.

'Bye,' said Anna.

George opened his mouth and closed it again.

Anna gave a nervous laugh. 'Hi!' she corrected hastily. 'I meant hi!' But she didn't.

For a few seconds Robert didn't move, frozen in bewilderment. Then he blinked, reached up to hang his coat on a hook, and coughed.

'I'm going to jump in the shower,' he said. 'Would you guys crack the window open for a bit? It's very smoky in here.'

'OK,' Anna said, far too brightly. 'Will do!'

She waited until he left the room, and rolled the dice. She and George watched them tumble across the game board and come to a stop on double sixes.

'Huh,' Anna said. 'Look at that.'

George made a face at her, brows arched, eyes wide, bemused and amused at once. *What the fuck?* he mouthed.

She shrugged.

Suspended over their unfinished game, they listened as Robert shuffled about in the bedroom, listened for his footsteps across the hallway and for the sound of the bathroom door closing. The pipes rattled and groaned tellingly when he ran the water in the shower.

'Oops,' George said.

'Fuck.'

'That was awkward.'
'It just came out. It was automatic.'
'I think the term is *subconscious*.'
'Fuck.'
'You gonna do something about it?'
Anna shrugged again.
'Oh come on!' George shouted, then lowered his voice. 'Just get it over with. Bite the bullet. Swallow the pill. But get it the fuck over with.'
'Yeah...'
'Grow some balls, little sister,' he counselled and then, uncharacteristically tender: 'You're better than this.'

Anna got up to open the window and watched the smoke gliding out, languidly, as the February chill seeped into the room. She shivered.

'That's enough,' she said, a few moments later, pushing the window shut. 'Shall we finish this game?'

'Nah,' said George, standing up. 'I'm gonna head off and leave you to it. Alright?'

'Alright.'

'Be brave,' he told her at the door, and although his smirk implied irony, the concern in his eyes was genuine. This would take courage, and it was long overdue.

Anna returned to the living room and stared at the backgammon pieces lined up on the board, suspended mid-game, and the double sixes that almost guaranteed her victory: wasted, because the next move would not be played. She slammed the set shut, sending the pieces clattering down the sides and hitting the bottom with a loud crash.

'Enough,' she said.

They had a perfectly pleasant evening. Anna made spaghetti carbonara and they sat down at the kitchen table together, unusually, to eat it. They even had a glass of wine and made some small talk – How was work today? What's new with George? – while they smoked their post-dinner cigarettes.

Anna got up to clear the table, while Robert sipped on his wine. She started doing the dishes then stopped, sponge in hand, and turned away from the sink to face Robert.

'This has to end,' she said. 'You know it, don't you?'

Apparently he didn't. He lowered his glass to the table, very slowly, but continued to hold it by the stem. Very slowly, he spoke:

'What has to end?'

'You and me, Robert. I'm sorry. It can't go on.'

Soapy water trickled down her hand and onto the floor, and she realised that, despite how composed she sounded, her fingers were tight around the sponge. She dropped it into the sink and wiped her hands on her jeans. 'We tried. We said we'd try. But it's not working. Is it?'

Robert stared straight ahead, glassy eyed. 'No,' he said, barely audible.

'It has to end. Tonight. I'm sorry.'

'Yes,' Robert said quietly. 'I'm sorry too.'

So it was amicable, after all. That night, not later. Later, it was acrimony and accusations and blame, the endless apportionment of guilt and blame, and not enough places to put them; it was poisoned words and barb wire comments and cold, brutal silences. But that night the words were gentle and there was a dignity to it, an unlikely grace, in the way they finally just let go. There was no tearing apart, no ripping, no resistance; there was nothing to hold them together, and they just stepped aside, and it was done. It was done, that night, this way, and it counted for something. It must have counted for something.

Anna abandoned the washing up and sat back down in her chair across the table from Robert. It was a small table, and she could easily reach over and touch his hand – but lightly, with the tip of a single finger resting on the edge of his fingernail, a loose connection. They stayed like that for a while, until Anna pressed her finger down on Robert's and drew her hand away.

'Shall I make us some coffee?' she suggested, mostly for something to say, something to do.

'No,' Robert said, shaking his empty wine glass. 'Let's drink.'

They dug out a bottle of vodka, almost full and left over from Anna's last birthday, and drank it neat, because they had neither mixers nor patience for getting drunk slowly. They poured it into shot glasses and before they brought the first one to their lips, Robert raised his glass, theatrically, and with a twisted smile proposed they drink to the end.

'To the end,' they both said, and clinked, and drank, wincing at the harsh taste of warm vodka. They slammed their glasses down, and filled them up again immediately, eager for the welcome numbness the next shot would bring.

'What are we drinking to this time?' Anna asked as she lifted her glass.

'To how we fucked up!' said Robert. They drank.

'To horrible heartbreak!' Anna called out for the next one.

'To being shit at relationships!'

Robert was funny that evening, with that cynical edge that Anna had always liked, and that counted for something: that she had liked him once and that she could like him still, after everything, if just for this final night. And if it was the last time that she felt this way, it didn't matter, because tonight he was gentle and thoughtful and honest and he made her laugh. He was a man who could say he was sorry, who could admit to having made mistakes and cry for what he'd lost. And he did, covertly, covering his face with his hands and dropping his head, while Anna cried openly and twice as much because the sight of Robert's shuddering shoulders would set her off again every time. This man who cried behind his hands and made jokes at his own expense was the kind of man she might have liked a lot more consistently, the kind of man she might have stayed with, if things had been different. If they had been different people.

'Is it because of Jack?' he asked, abruptly, late into the evening. There was a flatness to his voice as he said it, a resigned acceptance, and he kept his eyes fixed on the empty shot glass that he turned around and around in his hand.

'No,' Anna said quickly, instinct more than anything else. But although she owed Robert no debt, and there was nothing to be gained by last minute disclosures, the truth could not be a straight up "no". She revised it. 'Not directly.' It was the best she could do.

And Robert would hold it against her, later, this concession, this token truth, he would twist it and turn it ugly and treacherous and hurl it at her at every opportunity he found or created, but tonight he only nodded his head and poured them both another shot.

'To love,' he toasted, and the irony was that it was just as appropriate as it was ironic. Even in bitterness, there was a place for love.

So Anna raised her glass and looked Robert straight in the eyes, and they drank to love.

The next morning, subdued by their hangovers and the comforting absurdity of having held each other in bed through a largely sleepless night, they had strong cups of black coffee and a brief, civil discussion of the practicalities. Robert would move out, but there was no rush; Anna would relocate to the sofa and let him have the bed. They would split their joint belongings once Robert had found a flat and they knew what was there and what was missing. They wouldn't have sex, they decided, no matter what; they had almost fallen into it the night before, thrown together by their common sadness and reaching for solace in that one last time, but they had both been too emotionally drained to see it through. This was for the best, they agreed; they would stay friends. And then Robert got dressed and went to work, and Anna went back to bed, and cried.

She was shocked by how much it hurt, how it knocked her off her feet, how she found herself a broken thing on the floor, when she had expected to just stroll away from this, once it was done. She had thought doing it was the hard part. It had seemed easy the night before, too easy, but the relief she'd felt when she finally said the words – a few short words. What had taken her so long? – turned quickly and overwhelmingly to devastation. She was shocked at the violence of such a gentle parting, how hard it hit her, even before the violence actually began.

It didn't take long. As the shock wore off, so did Robert's affability, and dignity gave way to injured pride. It sprang up, roaring and swearing and threatening revenge, and set about rewriting history. Anna heard rumours that it was Robert who had left her, that she had been impossible to live with, that she had pleaded and begged, which she had neither energy nor interest to correct. Paradoxically, Robert often came home incensed by his own telling of these fictions, and accused her of having abandoned him.

'You brought me to this fucking place,' he'd scream or, worse, growl – an animal poised to attack, 'and then you dumped me. Just tossed me away.'

Yet you're still here, Anna would think, but she didn't say it. Most of the time, she said nothing. She could take the blame, all of it, if only he would take himself away.

But he stayed. Day after day, he was still there. He hated coming home to her, and yet he came back, night after night. He gave no sign of looking for a flat and, in a warped echo of their early days in Athens, Anna began circling ads in the papers for him.

'Look,' she'd say, with a forced enthusiasm that was increasingly manic, 'this one sounds promising!'

And Robert, when he deigned to cast his eyes over Anna's latest selections, would reject every single one, finding fault with the location, or the size, or the price or even, once, the syntax of the ad itself. He routinely charged her with ruthlessness, with selfishness, with trying to kick him out.

'You don't give a shit if I end up living in a dump,' he snarled. 'You just want me gone.'

One time, he flung the newspaper across the room, another time directly at Anna. But mostly he just ignored both Anna and the paper she was holding aloft, with that new, manic smile on her face, as if neither of them existed. Anna wondered if this was a symptom of denial or some other, unique stage of grief that Robert had invented himself, along with his version of the past they had shared and the end he had apparently instigated himself, and that Anna appeasingly described as consensual. Their uncontested parting, that Robert had turned into a contest, and won on a daily basis. Whatever it was, it manifested as complete and resolute inactivity, ads circled and unseen, newspapers piling up in the recycling bin in the kitchen. And the weeks went by, and Robert stayed.

The weeks went by, and Anna learned to duck and lie flat on the ground when Robert released another torrent of abuse and blame, and she finished her novel. She named it "Colourblind", wrote a cover letter and a synopsis and sent it off to agent after agent, and Robert smirked with every rejection letter that landed in their mailbox.

'Another one?' he'd mock. 'What a shame.'

Dylan asked to read the book.

'It's good,' he said, 'but your stories are better. Your stories are exceptional.'

'The *Jack* stories?'

'Yes. Why don't you send those off?'

'Nobody publishes short stories.'

'They do. They'll publish these.'

'But they're all about Jack. I call him Jack.'

'Then change his name. Call him Tom. But get them published.'

It took some adjusting to, this idea: to make what were essentially love letters to Jack public property. And the thought of calling him something else struck Anna as obscene. Disloyal, somehow. Wrong. But then again, she had no right to name him, to use his name in this way; any claim she might have had on him, she'd given up a long time ago. And he'd know himself, even by another name, but nobody else would know Tom. If the stories were published, if he read them, he'd know.

So Jack was renamed Tom and "Alternative Endings" sent off to a small, independent publisher in London that specialised in short stories.

And accepted.

Anna flew to London to meet her editor. She landed in Heathrow and as the plane broke through the cloud and made its final approach and the neat, flat fields of England came into view, the tiny Monopoly buildings and the motorways, the A roads and the toy cars, all dull and tinted grey under the dull grey English sky, Anna felt her heart crack open. She pressed her forehead against the window and cried, thick, silent tears that stung as she tried to hold them back, so as not to alarm her fellow passengers. And when the wheels hit the tarmac and the plane's engines roared as they made the transition from air to land, she thought *Well then. This is home.* It couldn't be anything else, the way it made her feel. She wiped her eyes, unbuckled her seatbelt, and made a decision. She turned to the woman in the seat next to her and smiled.

'It's exciting, isn't it?' the woman said. 'London!' It was her first time.

And Anna, who had made this journey dozens of times before, nodded.

'It is,' she said.

Her editor, Ben, met her by the receptionist's desk, offered her a cautious handshake and a cup of coffee, and led her to a small office with manuscripts piled high on the desk. He was a pale man in his mid-thirties, with fine, floppy hair, an anxious manner and an air of fragile awkwardness that reminded Anna, vaguely, of a character from the Dead Poet's Society. Perhaps it was deliberate. In any case, his undisguised enthusiasm for her work, the way his face became animated when he talked about what they'd do with it, floppy hair flapping everywhere and ink-stained hands drawing plans in the air, endeared him to Anna. He was a junior editor and she was his first author, and Anna liked that they were both novices, making their debut together.

Ben explained about editing and proofing and the author's role in this process, and publishing schedules.

'We're thinking November, if all goes well,' he told her. 'How does that sound?'

'Great,' Anna replied. It all sounded great.

He talked about advances, fees and royalties, launch dates and distribution and strategies for marketing and promotion. He asked Anna some questions, which she answered, but other than that she said very little, mostly because she couldn't quite believe this was happening. And as she left Ben's office and stepped back out into the cool dimness of the late April morning, all her excitement, her dazzlement, her disbelief, all of her gratitude converged into a single thought: *Jack. I need to tell Jack.*

She stayed with Laura. She was still in their old flat, but the flatmate who had replaced Anna had been replaced, in turn, by Julian, and what had once been her room was now their study, the double mattress on the floor swapped for a small sofa bed for guests to sleep in. It was strange for Anna to step back into her past and find it changed. Elsewhere, time passed. People moved on and redecorated and replaced you, if you went away. The gap you left was not so uniquely shaped as to remain a gap for long, impossible to fill except by your return. Life soon rises up and slots another shape into it, and moulds it to fit. Your place in the world is only yours while you occupy it, and then it's claimed by someone else. Was there a place for Anna here, still? Were there still cracks that she could slip into, if she came back?

Existential reflections aside, it was good to be back here, with Laura and Julian, sleeping on the sofa bed where her mattress had been, looking up at the same patch of ceiling. It was good to be away from her own sofa bed at home, away from the hostility and the bitterness that thickened the air in their flat and made it, sometimes, hard to breathe. Here, the sound of someone moving in the next room did not make her stomach lurch and her presence was relished rather than denied. Here, Laura fussed over her and Julian offered cups of tea and snacks from the kitchen cupboard and bounced around like a rubber ball, trying, simultaneously, to make Anna feel welcome and to stay out of their way. Here, the air was light and scented by Laura's laundry, a distinctive, comforting smell that Anna could never replicate despite using the same brand of washing powder. She had missed that smell. It was good to be back.

She only stayed for four days, but she managed to squeeze in a yoga class and a coffee with Ollie, and a whole day, the Saturday, with Toby and Lex. They met for lunch in Angel, and then caught the bus up to Highgate, to join Chris and Sylvia in the Woods, where they wheeled Amber down shady paths under the tall trees, her pushchair jerking and rattling and making her squeal with both fear and delight, and watched her stumble around the playground while they sipped takeaway coffees bought at the café. When Amber had had enough and her excitement turned to frustrated screeching and, before long, inconsolable howling, Chris and Sylvia took her home, and Toby, Lex and Anna walked up to Muswell Hill and spent the rest of the afternoon catching what sunshine remained in a pavement café on the Broadway. Chris and Sylvia rejoined them again in the evening, for dinner and drinks at the Slug & Lettuce, and Anna extracted promises from all of them, together and separately, that they wouldn't tell Jack that she was here. She knew she was pushing the boundaries of friendship by asking, getting their loyalties tangled up like a game of twister, but she couldn't see him and she didn't want him to know.
She had imagined meeting him; it was the first thing she'd thought about when this trip to London came up. She had imagined it like one of her dreams, sitting with him in a café somewhere and letting the day pass them by as they talked and fell silent, sank into that easy, restorative silence that only meant there was no need to talk. She saw

herself sitting next to him, floppy and surrendered, like she'd been spilled onto her seat, and looking up at his face. And she had imagined telling him her news, his eyes sparking up like fireworks set off into the sky to celebrate her success. He would say the perfect thing and he would smile at her and she would feel like everything in the world was exactly where it should be, and she couldn't bear it. She couldn't bear to see what she'd lost played out in the present, hers again briefly for a borrowed stretch of time, that she'd then have to give back, or owe. She didn't want to borrow: it had to be their time, or no time at all. She didn't want Jack giving her things that she couldn't keep.

So she got on a plane and flew back without seeing him. And she cried again as they glided off the runway, but this time she didn't look out of the window to see the cars and the buildings and the motorways and the fields getting smaller and disappearing in the haze of the clouds.

She called Jack as soon as she stepped out of the airport in Athens, back on Greek soil, so she wouldn't have to lie. She spoke to him while she smoked her first post-flight cigarette, which explained how light-headed she felt.

'I'm getting published,' she told him.

'Of course you are,' he said. He said the perfect things, and asked the perfect questions, and Anna smoked a second cigarette and then a third and paced up and down the crowded pavement outside the arrivals building and told him all about her book, everything, except what it was about.

'People,' she said vaguely, when he asked.

London only came up as a future prospect.

'Will you come for the launch?' he asked. 'You've gotta come! You've gotta go into a bookshop and see it! Can you imagine?' He was almost shouting, almost more excited than she was. This was why he was the one to call; this was what Jack did.

She couldn't help it: she laughed. 'That'll be amazing,' she admitted.

'So I guess I'll see you then.' There was an inflection to this phrase, the rise and fall of uncertainty. A question that Anna didn't know how to answer.

'OK,' she said.

'If you want.'

'OK.'

She smoked one more cigarette after they said goodbye, sitting down on a bench with her rucksack on her knees, reluctant to break the spell. Preparing herself for the journey into town, and home.

A few days after her return, Robert summoned her to the kitchen – neutral territory – for "a chat". He offered to make coffee, which Anna refused.

'This may be hard to hear,' he began (he seemed quite happy about it), 'but I've met a woman.'

'Good for you,' Anna replied.

'It's quite serious,' Robert pressed. 'She really *understands* me.' This clearly wasn't going the way he'd imagined.

'Does that mean you'll be moving out?'

'Of course I'll be moving out!' he snapped, the soft, patronising tone abandoned. 'You think I enjoy living here like this, with *you?*'

'You don't seem to mind, seeing as it's been two months.'

'It's not that easy,' he retorted, reverting to petulance. 'But I'll be out of your way soon, don't worry about it. I'm moving on. With my woman.'

'Excellent,' Anna said flatly. 'Just don't bring her here.'

It was obvious, from the look that twitched across Robert's face, that he already had. Fucked her in their bed, the bed that she'd built for them, while Anna was away. She was surprised by how little it mattered. She smiled, a touch cruelly, at his discomfort.

'I'm glad we had this *chat*,' she said, standing up and leaving the room. Robert didn't move from the kitchen table for a long time.

Lex called, and she said 'I'm sorry' before she said 'hello.'

'I told Jack about London,' she confessed. 'We saw him last night and he kept talking about your book, so I thought he knew. Toby *hates* me! Do you hate me?'

'I don't hate you. What did he say?'

'Not a lot actually, he just looked kind of sad. So I panicked and told him it was probably because you were going through some stuff and didn't want to complicate it by seeing him. And he said what stuff, all concerned, so I blurted it out, about Robert.' She had barely taken a breath throughout this whole account, so she paused now to fill her lungs. 'That you split up,' she added.

'And?'

'And nothing. He asked if you were OK, and then nothing. He went off somewhere for a while, probably to the bar, and then he came back and started talking about something else. A new contract he just got, I think. And Toby had shouted at me in the meantime, so I didn't press it. Are you sure you don't hate me?'

'I'm sure. It's OK. No harm done.'

But it was ironic that, out of the four promises made, it was Lex, whose allegiance, if questioned, would be incontestably with Anna, who had given her away. And, in the light of what happened, Anna only wished she'd done it sooner, while she was still in London. If only she'd seen Jack then, after all. But neither of them could have known – when Anna asked for a promise, when Lex made it and broke it – what the consequences would be. They couldn't have known. But harm was done.

*

We've just gone into the second week of May and I think Athens knows I'm planning to leave it, because the weather's been consistently glorious every single day since my return from London (the contrast: such different definitions of spring) almost two weeks ago. I'm still in bed, but I can see the sky through the window and there's not a smudge of cloud on it, only a flawless, unbroken postcard-blue. I'm still in bed, though it's gone ten o'clock; I've no lessons until the afternoon, and Robert stayed out last night, so I'm savouring the rare sensation of solitude, the healing veil of silence that's settled over the flat, the absence of tension, the looseness of my limps as I lie, stretched out, on my sofa bed. A heated rectangle of sunshine frames my feet and makes promises of summer. Athens is throwing all it's got at me, but I didn't choose London for the weather. I will forsake this cunning, sunny city once again, for another: the one that makes me cry. Dirtier, darker and dangerous, but it's staked its claim on me and it's calling me home.

The phone brings me back to my bed, and the name it displays, improbably, is Jack. I let it ring three times, quiver impatiently in the palm of my hand as I stare at it, excited and terrified at once, before I answer.
'Hello?'
'Anna,' he breathes, a little raspy, and needlessly, since he's the one who called me.
'Yes,' I say, equally pointless.
'What are you doing?'
'Not much,' I reply warily. 'I'm lying in bed, looking out the window. It's very bright. You should see the sky.'
'I am.'
'You what?'
'I'm looking at the sky.'
'Oh. OK.' I'm really confused by this phonecall.
'In Athens,' he says.
'I'm sorry?'

'I'm looking at the sky in Athens.' A pause. 'I'm at the airport.'

'In Athens.'

'In Athens.'

'Um. What? How?'

He doesn't answer that. 'Want to have coffee?' he says instead. 'I know a place in town.'

I have no recollection of getting dressed and leaving the house. I must have brushed my teeth, showered, given some thought to what I'd wear, I must have called my students and cancelled my lessons, but I don't know about any of these things. All I know is that I'm walking down the hill, carefully, down the steep, treacherous streets that lead into the centre of town. I'm walking towards Jack and it's a very self-conscious act, the placing of one foot in front of the other, connecting to the ground and lifting my heels and bending my knees to keep this action going, to keep going, walking to where Jacks awaits. There must be thoughts going round in my head, questions and implications, but I don't know.

We meet in a café in Monastiraki, overlooking the railway lines, that we'd discovered one summer, his first time in Athens. Years ago. We liked it, then, for its unlikely bordered tranquillity – potted plants drawing a perimeter around the tables – amidst the busyness, for the tourists that passed and pointed and shook out maps, for the rumble of the passing trains, for the ancient bulk of the Acropolis on the other side of the tracks. I haven't been since moving back to Athens, I wouldn't take Robert there, but I've passed it and I know it's still open.

I'm surprised Jack remembers where it is, after all this time, but he's there when I arrive, leaning against the chicken wire fence on the opposite side of the street, with his back to the railway tracks and a small rucksack by his feet. The sun is in his eyes and they're half closed, his head angled up to the sky. A train rumbles past, but he doesn't move. He doesn't see me until I'm standing right in front of him, and then he opens his eyes, unhurriedly, and lowers his head and looks at me, as if he knew I was there all along.

We smile. We don't touch.

'Well,' I say. 'Here you are.'

'Here I am.'

I wait for him to elaborate, but he doesn't. He only nods towards the café, and I follow him, dodging the tourists and their maps, across the street. We find a table in the sunshine, not shaded by the awning, and we both drag our chairs closer to the corner, crowding in around it, before we slip into our seats. Our knees brush against each other and neither of us pulls away.

And it's how I imagined, with the talking and the silences intermingled and the warmth of his knee against mine and the slowness of everything: exactly how I knew it would be. And the cost: that I'll have to leave this bubble eventually, and enter, again, the world of other people, where things move too fast and nothing makes much sense. Nothing makes as much sense as this.

'I'm sorry about London,' I say, hours later. 'I know Lex told you. It's just that...'

But Jack lifts his hand off the table: stop. 'You don't need to explain. It's OK. I get it.'

'You do?'

He nods. 'I think so. I do. But then again – here I am.'

'Here you are.' I still don't know what it means. I want to ask, to question the contradiction, but something stops me – cowardice, the possibility of an answer I won't like, or of the one I will, the one I dare not hope for – and Jack speaks again.

'And – your boyfriend,' he says.

'Yeah. That's over.'

And he doesn't ask either. Neither of us asks the questions we should, to get the answers we need. Neither of us knows, yet, that we need them. We have our talk and our silence, our coffees and our sunshine and our knees pressed together and we are drowsy and careless. He doesn't ask and I'm relieved, because I don't want Robert breaking into this moment, I don't want to talk about him to Jack and I would, if he asked. The moment is ours, alone, and the moment after it's too late. Because what Jack does next is look down and stare at his hands, his fingers splayed out on the table, gripping the edge, and I feel his knee pushing against mine, not subtle anymore but urgent, demanding, and when he looks up again everything explodes and I literally have no breath in my body, and I know what he's here for and I forget what the question was.

I also forget to pay but luckily Jack remembers and he takes care of it, laughing with the waitress, while I stand, dazed, by the table, waiting for him to collect me and lead me out. We still haven't touched, except for our knees.

We leave the café and turn left, arbitrarily, and walk along the tracks, until we come to the end of the road, and I realise I don't know where we're going. Jack must be thinking the same because he stops short, at the same time I do, and we look at each other, nervous and brave and suddenly shy.

'Home?' he suggests, in a low, scratchy voice that I can hardly hear over the hubbub of the street, but I can read his lips, and his eyes sparkle with stars.

'Yes,' I say, soaring one second and crashing the next, when I remember. 'But Jack, you should know. Robert's still there.'

'Oh,' Jack says, and the stars fall out and scatter, flickering, on the dirty pavement by our feet, and go dim. I want to pick them up, put the light back into them and have them rise again in his eyes, have him look at me that way again, but I don't know how. I try to explain.

I don't say it's awful. I don't say fuck, you can't imagine what it's like. I don't say please come and beat this guy to a pulp, please come and throw him out of my flat and then stay. I say the worst thing I can, under the circumstances. I say: 'It's complicated.'

And Jacks nods as if he understands, but he doesn't. Of course he doesn't. And I should know this, but I don't. And harm is done.

'We can go,' I continue, 'but it might be a bit awkward.' Thinking: I told Robert not to bring her. Thinking: not the same – this is Jack. Thinking: fuck it, I'm taking him home. 'Let's go,' I decide.

But Jack doesn't move. 'I think,' he says slowly, 'maybe not.'

So we don't go, and Jack never sees the sofa bed, opened up to the middle of the room, rug and coffee table pushed aside; unmade, sheets crumpled, as I left them this morning. He never sees the clothes and shoes I've moved into the living room and the hallway so I don't have to go into the bedroom, piles of clothes folded up on chairs, shoes and sandals lined up along the walls, the plastic bag that contains my underwear. He never sees the bedroom that is clearly only Robert's, the balled up white socks and sports' papers and filmed over cups of tea strewn across the floor, the spray-on deodorant and the plate full of crumbs on the dresser. He never sees Robert, emerging, when he hears us come in, from the kitchen or the bedroom, and probably making some caustic, cutting remark about the two of us, about how it had been about Jack all along, before storming out or, worse, staying. He never sees the look that would be in his eyes, the coldness, the separation, that would tell him what he needed to know; he never sees Robert and me together, in the same room and as apart as two people can be, so he would understand. We don't go, and Jack doesn't see. He never sees any of it, how I really live.

We follow the tourists up to Plaka and find a hotel just off the main shopping street, a middle range one, ugly-modern and the lights in the reception too harsh, shining off too many reflective surfaces, but we're looking for neither quaintness nor luxury. There is a room with a door we can close, there is a bed with crisp, clean sheets, and an electric kettle, and our requirements are fulfilled. We get a little bit excited as we ride the lift up to our floor and search out our room; if we put aside the circumstances that brought us here, this – checking into a hotel spontaneously, with the sun still shining outside – feels like an adventure, vaguely naughty, and it makes us giggle. If we put everything aside, this is me and Jack and it cannot be wrong. And we can do that, we can put it all aside, and the stiffness that took hold of us before, the first awkward silence in all of our years, that trailed us from that street corner in Monastiraki all the way to this hotel, loses its grip and we make faces at each other in the lift, race down the dim-lit hallway and crash, loose-limbed and laughing now, into our room. Jack dumps his rucksack in a corner by the window, and we bounce around, opening drawers and cupboards and wardrobe doors, checking out the hangers and the spare pillows, the hairdryer and the shoe horn, exclaiming at the toiletries in the bathroom. Jack flicks through Greek TV channels that he finds hilarious, and I fling teabags at him, for no particular reason.

And then suddenly it's serious, and there's a different kind of tension as we finally touch. We meet in the middle of the room and put our hands on each other, grip each other's shoulders, arm's length apart, like an awkward school party slow dance, except we don't move, at all. Jack looks at me and I look at him and we lock into each other, and I feel it building up, rising up from my belly, first a tingle and a flutter and then a huge, rushing, roaring wave, swelling up and spilling over and I literally ache for his whole body against mine. I shudder, once. And now we dance, twisting and stepping until we find the bed and then, finally, his weight, his heat, hard bones and soft skin, his jagged breath on my face; finally, mercifully, his lips against mine. And I am lost. I have just lost every game I've ever played, and the years I spent looking for other places, when there was nowhere else I could belong. I am lost, because I won't come back from this.

This, soft groans and taut muscles and clothes ripped from our bodies and skin against skin; this new, familiar thing that our bodies remember, that we tried to forget, and how easily we slot back into each other, easily but not gently, with a new, sharp, imperative hunger, because it's been too long; this, Jack finally, mercifully, back inside me and me grasping, pulling him closer, deeper, and his hips digging into my thighs and my legs wrapped around his waist, with our gazes fastened, and we never close our eyes, not once – we never look away. And the stillness: that we move against each other, with each other, into each other, and it's stillness. This. Not moving on, not moving away; I have been everywhere else, and this is where I belong, still, moving, with Jack.

But in the stillness, something stirs. As we lie together, after, interwoven, as we lie side by side holding hands, as we lie facing each other, our noses touching, sharing one breath; as we take turns and take our time to run our hands over one another's body, to take each other in, slowly now, carefully, coming together and drawing apart so we can look at each other again; as we lie still, twisted into one, holding on – something stirs. And even in hindsight, I can't claim that I sense it. There is, perhaps, an undercurrent of unease, pinpricks of it, but I am tingling all over with Jack's presence and I don't know it. I don't recognise it, that something is wrong, but something is wrong because the morning comes and Jack leaves. And even in hindsight, I don't understand how I let him.

Morning comes and we know it by the light sifting through the slit between the curtains. We haven't slept, not really, only snatches of it here and there; we didn't want to miss any of it, give any time away to sleep. We didn't want to close our eyes. I get up and throw the curtains open and let the sunshine in; Jack squints and wrinkles up his face as the brightness hits his eyes, and I'm swept up by such a rush of tenderness that it almost floors me. I climb back into bed and drape myself over him, with my ear pressed against his chest and my hand lifted up to shade his eyes. I listen to his heartbeat and try to match it to my own, but it's a little slower, a fraction of a second behind. I wonder if I could catch up with him, if there's a way I could control my heart and bring us into sync. But I've forgotten what it means when someone has your heart: that it's his bidding that it does.

    'I should probably think about making a move,' he says, and my heart stops.

'A move,' I stammer, stupidly, 'to where?'

'The airport.'

I lower my hand and the sun blasts into his eyes and he angles his head away as I raise myself up to look at him. His face is very still.

'Oh,' I hear myself say, steadily, like a person who still has a heart that beats. 'I didn't realise you were going back today. What time's your flight?'

He doesn't reply.

'Jack? What time?'

'I don't know.'

I slide off him and onto the mattress and, freed of my weight, Jack sits up, on the edge of the bed. Hands on his knees, feet planted on the floor. He stares directly at the wall.

'I don't understand. How can you not know?'

'I didn't book a return. I'll just go there and catch the next flight out.' He says these words as if it's normal, as if it's possible that he's actually saying them.

I don't understand.

Jack turns around then, twists himself all the way around to find my eyes and hold them. He waits.

I say: 'OK.' Even in hindsight, I don't know why. All of the words I could have said, words swollen with love, emboldened by love, brave words that could have stopped him, of all the words I wanted to say, why I chose this impotent, empty one. When I could have stood up and simply said 'No'. How is it, when I had the hindsight of what it means to lose Jack, that I surrendered to losing him again?

And now he looks away, a tiny shift of the gaze, away from mine. I do not hold him anymore. And I think: perhaps this is justice. Retribution. Tit for tat, an eye for an eye. Perhaps this is a circle, closed.

Jack rises to his feet, picks up his rucksack and pads into the bathroom without a word. He closes the door.

I retrieve two teabags from the floor and make two cups of tea, empty a miniature tin of condensed milk into each one and two sachets of sugar in Jack's, and stir and stir and stir, letting myself be lulled by this repetitive, mindless action and the tinkle of the spoon against the sides. I leave both cups on the sideboard by the kettle and watch the steam rise and curl. When Jack comes out, showered and dressed, I point him to his cup, my meagre offering that I cannot deliver to him because my hands are shaking and I don't want him to see.

He walks over and touches his lips to the side of my head. I feel the warmth of his breath before he pulls away.

'Thanks,' he says, and takes a sip of his tea. I don't touch mine.

I take him to the airport and we sit in the new silence as the train rattles up the tracks, too fast, and a stern female voice announces station after station like a countdown. Our knees knock into each other as the carriage jerks, but it's accidental this time. At the departures hall, we scan the board for the next flight to London and I follow Jack, wobbling like a puppet with its strings cut off, to the airline desk to buy his ticket. There are tender places all over my body, bruises in the making, that would normally make me smile, make me close my eyes and breathe a deep sigh and shiver at the memory of how he put them there, but all my smiles today are just mimicry, remembered behaviour, and the sighs are only an attempt to get some air into my lungs.

I perform one of those smiles now, as he brandishes his boarding pass and says 'Just in time', as though we're in a world where getting on that flight – the first flight out of here – is a good thing. I don't know this place. I follow him, lost, to that terrible, final stop, where poles and stretched-out belts delineate the route to the passport control booths. We come to a standstill.

How is it that I let him walk away? When he is still here, now, standing in front of me? I should wrap myself around him, I should say *don't go, where is it that you want to go to?* I should snatch the boarding card from him and tear it into a thousand pieces and throw it over the both of us like confetti and tell him he's not going anywhere. Instead I raise my hand, unsteadily, still shaking, and aim it in his direction, but I no longer know which parts of him I'm allowed to touch so I clutch his elbow and hold. And for a moment our eyes connect again and with a jolt I know that no matter what it looks like this is not the final scene, but then Jack blinks and drops his gaze and I let go of his elbow and he turns around and joins the queue.

When they come up, when they blossom on my skin, my bruises will be a map of everywhere he touched me, everything he did to me the night before. Half the story: the other half Jack is taking with him, written on his own skin. And I let him. I follow him with my eyes, only my eyes, as he shuffles up the queue, as he reaches the booth, as he hands his passport over and slips to the other side, out of sight, out of reach. I follow him but I don't move. Not for a long time. Not until I start noticing the strange looks I'm attracting and a lady in an airport uniform comes over and asks me, kindly, to step out of the way.

'You could take a seat,' she suggests, and points to a row of metal benches behind me. And I do, for a while, because I can't think of where to go.

I am lost, and I don't know how to get back. And the map will only lead us anywhere if we bring the two halves together again, side by side. It's the only way it can be read.

Eleven

Getting back to London was easy enough, no more than a string of practicalities, and Anna did it quietly, without any fuss. She gave the flat up to Robert, leaving everything behind, everything bought to furnish that aborted attempt at a life together. She didn't want any of it, no mementos and no negotiations; Robert made a few heart-hearted offers of cash for the more expensive items, but she declined, politely. Not out of generosity: this, at least, was something she could move on from, and she wanted nothing of it following her to wherever she ended up next. She took only the things she'd brought, most of them boxed up and waiting to be shipped back to London.

She moved into George's spare room for the summer, and shared it with his desk and his computer, four speakers, an amp, a subwoofer and a mixing deck, the single futon she slept on barricaded in by all these black machines, looming at various heights around her, but she had more space now than the last few months in her spacious living room. She used the amp as a bedside table, to hold her book and her ashtray, and sometimes played music as loud as she could get away with, with the bass turned right up, and let it vibrate through her body as she lay on her futon; it felt therapeutic, somehow.

She took June and July to put her affairs in order, tidy up before going away, serving out her notice at the yoga studio and wrapping up her lessons. A couple of her students, the more advanced ones, whose lessons mostly took the form of conversation, suggested they carry on over skype, and Anna made arrangements with them to try it out once she was settled. Her spare time she gave to friends and family, stocking up on coffees and drinks, lunches, dinners, walks and conversations to take with her back to London, where she'd have to get used to missing them all over again. She and George spend many evenings sharing the sofa or the floor, listening to music and not saying very much, evenings when they still took each other for granted and no effort had to be made, and Anna savoured these more than anything. As soon as she left, any time she had with these people – her brother, her parents, her friends – would count as precious. It would have to be meted out carefully, divided equally among them so they all got enough, though it would never feel that way. Anna knew: she had done this before. There would be no more casual evenings, and that was the cost of being split between two cities, living your life in two places at once. The first time you leave, the meter starts running, clocking up lost time, adding to your debt.

Anna had done this before, but it was different this second time around. Moving to London at eighteen, with a single suitcase and very little baggage, with Cat and with teenage dreams of freedom and independence, underground bars and interesting people on the brink of being made real, she had no concept of leaving anything behind. Nothing to look back on. There had been tears at the airport, but their eyes were dry before they'd reached their gate. Neither of them had cried leaving Greece again, but they had both sobbed, inconsolably and publicly, when they flew out of London, their first Christmas back. And then tactlessly told their parents when they met them, eager and emotional, on the other end. No concept.

There would be no tears this time either, even though this departure was more final than any other before; all of them had become hardened by many years of coming and going and these airport partings were almost routine. But she would look back to see them, this time, whoever came to send her off, as they stood, a little stiffly, dried-eyed and accepting on the other side of the barriers; she would raise her hand and nod her head, before turning away.

It hadn't been easy, explaining, gaining their acceptance if not their understanding. Everyone had assumed that Anna coming back meant that she was staying, though she had made no such promise, and they felt, now, that she wasn't simply leaving, but leaving them behind. Unchosen. Because moving to London at thirty-one was a choice; moving to London a second time, after two years in Athens, was permanent. And Anna was all too aware of the implications, of choosing that over this, one set of people over another to share the everyday, unremarkable moments with, the casual evenings, the effortless, meaningless chats. Her conversations with these people, who nodded sadly but with understanding, would now forever be confined to catching up.

Nobody had given her too hard a time. Even the friends who tried to talk her round, who pointed out, a little defensively, the good things about Athens, could see that Anna didn't belong in this city. She had stood with one foot in the river Thames all these years, trying to keep her balance as the tides swept in and out, and it was time she placed them both on firmer ground.

And Cat knew that better than anyone, but she had been the hardest to tell. Even harder when Anna realised that, despite her assumption that Cat – tough, courageous, independent, who'd managed to turn this place around so it fit her – didn't really need her, she was nearly as scared as Anna was. She had taken the news quietly, as if she'd been expecting it.

'But I can't imagine being here without you,' she said, exactly as Anna had years ago in London, when the opposite move was being discussed. 'I've never had to do it before.'

And they both fell silent because there was nothing, this time, to be done. Cat wouldn't follow her back to London and Anna couldn't stay, and they would have to find a way to keep their lives connected while they lived them apart. They'd never had to do it before, and they would have to learn, and that was the cost of the freedom they'd claimed, thirteen years ago, when they climbed onto that first plane together, and the meter started ticking up their debt.

They spent ten days together in Paros, an echo of the previous summer but with the sound turned low, just Anna, Cat and Dylan and the long, hot August days, scented by the sea and tinged with the slow, soft melancholy of good things that will end too soon. It was an undemanding feeling, a nostalgia in advance, that lingered unobtrusive at the edges of everything they did, nudging Anna gently, every so often, to bring her attention to another memory being made. There was a cost to this, too, a down payment on things she had yet to miss, on the moments she'd miss in the future, away from this house, this restaurant, this beach, and Anna tried to collect as many of them as she could, stuff her pockets full of them, pebbles from a beach, flowers pressed between the pages of a book, to add to her reserves.

She landed with both feet back on British soil on a Friday afternoon in late August, carrying things much heavier than the two suitcases she dragged behind her, but there was a lightness in every one of her steps as she walked the long corridor that led to the exit and the smoking area. It was a warm, dry afternoon, hazy sunshine and harmless clouds, and Anna stood between her two suitcases, one on either side, and smoked and gazed at the sign that said "A WARM WELCOME: *Gatwick*", and smiled. 'Thank you,' she mouthed. She had never liked Gatwick but she loved it today; today, it welcomed her home, with warmth.

She launched her second life in London at Notting Hill Carnival. She had timed her arrival deliberately, to coincide with the Bank Holiday weekend and the colourful, chaotic street party that marked the end of summer and the city fading back into grey. It was a tradition she'd skipped, year after year, every year promising she'd definitely go the next until the years ran out, and it now felt like a rite of passage that she ought to undertake, an appropriate way to begin anew. She mentioned this idea to Lex, a veteran carnival goer, who took it upon herself to serve as Anna's guide and priestess, in a pair of metallic emerald green leggings, a feather in her hair, smudges of colour on her cheeks and whistle on a rainbow string dangling from her neck.

They met at Queensway station and Lex laid down the rules, which Toby punctuated with grave nods. 'Don't lose me,' she warned, stern-faced. 'And don't even think about needing to pee. Do you need to pee?'

Anna shook her head, poked at her bladder to make sure, and shook her head again.

'Excellent. Let's do it!' She grabbed Toby's hand, and set off up the road, and Anna trotted dutifully after them, feeling brand new, less of a Londoner that when she'd first arrived.

They watched the floats rolling by from the corner of Westbourne Grove, and then got swept up by the crowds and jostled through a maze of unrecognisable streets, past the sound systems blasting out bass-heavy beats and the stalls selling Rastafarian paraphernalia to a variety of over-excited white Londoners. Anna ate jerk chicken, rice and peas and a doughy fried dumpling the size of her fist, shared a spliff with Lex and Toby, sprawled out, a little self-consciously, in a valley between two mountains of discarded food containers, stained napkins and beer bottles on the pavement of what, on Tuesday, would once again revert to a quiet residential street, and danced, in passing, to some reggae until the river of bobbing heads and twitching limbs spat her back out onto Westbourne Grove, as the light faded to a rare, pink dusk. There, she said goodbye to Lex and Toby, who had offered to see her out before heading back in. Lex leant in to hug her, pressing her face against Anna's and rocking her gently from side to side.

'Welcome back,' she said as she drew away, and blew, once, on her whistle. Some of her face paint rubbed off onto Anna's cheek, but she didn't know it until she got home.

After two weeks of staying at Laura and Julian's, and seeing countless dark, dank bedsits, windowless, airless, joyless and provocatively overpriced, that made her soul shrink with pre-emptive despair, Lex suggested she sublet her studio in Seven Sisters so she could go live with Toby on a trial basis. Anna moved in, and made a home out of

Lex's things, with small touches of her own provided by the few items she'd brought along in her suitcases, squeezed in amongst her clothes, in a studio much like the one she'd rented post Jack. She didn't miss the irony of this, nor was she surprised when she found herself back in her leggings, greeting clients through a could of incense smoke, two mornings and two evenings a week, a way to fill her time and pay her rent while she waited for her book to be launched. Ollie had been gracious enough when she turned up one morning, sheepish, and asked for a job, and he had shown exemplary restraint while they discussed the terms of her return, only mentioning her degrees and her "lady writer" status once. The professional act was dropped as soon as he had her trapped behind the desk, with a new name badge pinned to her top, and never missed an opportunity to cackle some variation of "they all come crawling back" as he passed her – which wasn't true, because Lex had left soon after Anna to be a yoga teacher, and only ever walked through the door, fully upright, to teach her weekly class. But as it applied to her own circumstances, Anna couldn't argue. She wasn't surprised because, although she couldn't say where she was going, she'd sensed something inherently cyclical in the way she moved, an inevitable trajectory that kept her in orbit around a far away, fantastical sun. She wasn't surprised, but she did wonder at the perversity of humans, who only appreciated what they had after they'd gone to all kinds of trouble to dismantle it and trample on it and give it away, dazzled by some shiny new thing that caught their eye, and twice the trouble to retrieve all its scattered, flattened pieces and put it back together again, a second hand, patched-up version of what they had before, that they could now be grateful for. And Anna couldn't fail to see the irony, that she was one of them and she was grateful, but if she'd ended up exactly where she'd begun there was probably a reason for it.

It wasn't Jack. Jack was the reason for a lot of things, but not for this. This she had to try to do without him, for herself. She didn't contact him; she didn't tell him she was back. She preferred to imagine that their time had yet to come, that there was still a one day that belonged to them, somewhere up ahead, and they hadn't wasted it on that night in Athens. That whatever harm they had done that evening, whatever damage it was that they had caused wasn't irreparable. She preferred to imagine than to act, than to pick up the phone and call him and risk hearing his voice flat, drained of pleasure or love, than to see him and to find that he had erased her from his eyes. She preferred to imagine than to know. She stopped looking for reasons in the past, and found reasons to be happy in the present. She kept herself busy, in the new, familiar life she'd patched together from the old. She kept herself in orbit, a ship going round and round in the sky until it's called back down to earth.

Alternative Endings

It is an odd shaped bit of paper, a triangle with one jagged edge, a corner torn hastily off a flyer or a leaflet. "Jayne", it says, followed by a number; it has been written in eyeliner, dark brown, smudged but clear. Undeniable. It has come out of Tom's pocket.

I am always nagging him about emptying out his pockets on the bedside table, all these random items that I don't know what to do with cluttering it up and leaving no space for my book and my phone. They get knocked off onto the floor and kicked about, and then we have to crawl around looking for them under the bed and in the corners, when Tom suddenly remembers some important receipt, and I'm not allowed to say I told you so. It drives me crazy.

It's a USB stick this time, and a lighter and a foil wrapper from a sweet. And this crumpled piece of paper with its smudged but unmistakable message. It's the eyeliner that gets me, and that crooked, jagged edge. The urgency they imply, and I see her, this Jayne, who cannot wait to give my boyfriend her phone number, ripping a corner off whatever piece of paper she can get her hands on, and rummaging in her clutch for her eyeliner pen. I feel sick.

I sit down heavily on the bed, holding the bit of paper by the edges; I don't want her eyeliner on my fingers. I think of the night before, when Tom was out without me. Some work thing, the launch of a new internet service that he had been involved in designing, but I wanted to go to a yoga class and couldn't be bothered to travel into town after. I think about the last few weeks, how Tom has been unusually quiet, a little withdrawn, and I add it all together and come up with a hundred women, a hundred eager Jaynes who wear eyeliner and low cut tops and lurk in dark places pouting provocatively while I do my yoga, oblivious, always ready to fling my boyfriend their number, and run their long red nails down his chest. This is the mathematics of fear, and it doesn't jump to conclusions: it leaps and it throws itself frantically against walls.

I wait for Tom to come home. I hear the twist of his key in the lock, the creak and the click of the door, the heavy, tired footsteps. I don't move from the bed. I haven't moved since I found it, at least two hours ago.

'Anna?' he calls out, and pads into the bedroom. 'Are you OK?'

'Should I be worried about this?' I ask, and hold out my hand.

He glances down at it, the paper-thin proof of my cruel, paranoid science resting in my palm and he says 'No', and I nod my head as if this is enough, but I search for satisfaction in this answer and it's empty. But it's the question, I realise, that's flawed, not the answer.

'Why do you have it?' I try again.

'This girl gave it to me last night. I meant to throw it away. Where did it come from?'

'It was in your pocket,' I say. 'It was right there.' He follows my finger to where I'm pointing, accusatory, to the place where I found it, next to our bed.

'Sorry,' he says, then: 'Oh. You *are* worried.'

I nod. 'You've been weird with me lately. And this.'

'This is just a piece of paper.' He takes it from me, crushes it in his hand and tosses it behind his back. 'Gone,' he says. 'Never worry. But I'm sorry. I guess I've been too caught up in this launch. Was I weird?'

'Quiet. Kind of distant.'

'It was a tough project. I didn't mean to. But did you really think I'd – what? Cheat on you?'

I shrug and look up at him, pleading.

'Baby,' he says. 'You're crazy.' He comes closer and wedges himself between my knees, and he looms over me, smiling, magnificent: my boyfriend. The best man I've ever met. The most solid, the most honest. Whatever I might find, whatever I might go looking for, he's never given me reason to doubt.

I hook my fingers in the waistband of his jeans and tug, gently. Another, different plea. And Tom lowers himself down as I slip my hands beneath his top and find skin, and pushes me back onto the bed and eases his hips between my legs. I rip his top off, more urgent that any Jayne could ever be, and run my short, unpainted fingernails down his chest. He looks at me and I have all the answers.

'I'm crazy about you,' he says. 'Never worry.' After that, it's a long time before we speak.

***

35 years, a celebration, and I go rogue. I bake a cake, chocolate, with the icing dyed blue, for Boo, and stud it with candles, the classic stripy ones, in pink plastic holders. Tom frowns when he sees it, when I come out from the kitchen to the tune of all our friends singing happy birthday, with the forbidden cake all lit up, and he berates me with a look, but I'm not sorry: this is a celebration.

'Make a wish!' everyone urges, and he complies, squeezing his eyes closed and scrunching his whole face up, and making little jagged lines, like cartoon lightning bolts, appear across his forehead. But there are no storms in this man.

'What did you wish for?' I ask, once he's dutifully blown the candles out.

'I wished that you won't do this again,' he says in a stern tone, but his eyes smile.

'Can't promise you that,' I reply defiantly. 'We have too much to celebrate. Do you forgive me?'

'Always.'

The cake has not risen well and it's a bit doughy inside, but the icing is delicious and soon enough we're all licking it off knives and spoons and scraping it off with our fingers. We dance, high on sugar and loosened by alcohol, daredevils in the garden under a low, heavy sky that's about to crack open, sticky all over as we wade through the thick, humid air that foretells a summer storm. Tom and I hold onto each other and stumble around, in a tipsy imitation of a romantic dance, until I break away to get another beer from the kitchen. I watch him when I return, from a distance, at the far end of the garden, swaying to the music as he chats to a couple of his friends from work, and I feel how I always feel when I stop and look at him and take it all in: awe and gratitude and pride and that electric tingle that I know is love.

We have too much to celebrate, much more than a birthday. We have too much to be grateful for. Nine months ago, I almost walked away from this. I waited behind our door, waited for the scrape of Tom's key in the lock, and I was ready to say goodbye as he said hello. I took a deep breath and prepared to say the words that would end it. But then Tom walked in, and he smiled when he saw me, waiting for him behind the door. And the thought of doing something that would mean I wouldn't see this again – Tom coming home, smiling – was unbearable. Impossible. The thought that I had almost done it: impossible.

Later, when the storm has broken and we're lying in bed, surrounded by the debris of the party and listening to the rain pounding horizontally against our windows, I turn on my side and burrow into his armpit, as he lies facing the ceiling with his hands behind his head.

'I almost left a few months ago,' I tell him, muffled, lips moving against his skin.

'I know. I could feel it.'

'Why didn't you say anything?'

'Why didn't you?'

'I was scared.'

He unfolds his arms and reaches down to my hips, and draws me close so I'm draped over one half of him, and my head slots into the crook of his neck. Then he folds his arms again across my back. Enfolds me.

'Don't ever be scared,' he says. 'There's nothing to be scared of.'

'I was scared I might lose you,' I confess, in my smallest voice.

'Never.' His arms tighten around me, and I can feel the words vibrating in his throat. 'Not possible.'

Exactly.

***

I wait behind the door for Tom to come home. I have to be here, in position, to lie in wait, like a predator ready to pounce. If he walks in and kicks his shoes off, if he drops his bag by the door, if he pads into the living in his socks, if he falls back on the sofa and stretches his arms over his head and sighs with the relief of being home, I will lose my nerve. If he smiles at me, I will forget what I mean to say, the phrases I've been practising all afternoon, every afternoon, since I found that bit of paper that turned worry into doubt.

The key turns in the lock and the doors creaks open. The door creaks and it needs oiling, but that's not my problem anymore. Once I've said the words, it will no longer be my door. I catch a glimpse of Tom's face as he pushes in, shoulder first, and his lips begin the journey towards a smile. I crush it.

'Tom,' I say. 'I'm done. I can't do this anymore. It's over.'

His face freezes for a few seconds before his lips drop down into a hard, straight line. He fixes his eyes on me, takes another step into the house and pushes the door shut with his foot.

'No,' he says simply. 'No.'

I'm not prepared for this. I expected silence, acceptance, a departure; I had prepared for these like I'd prepared the words I'd say, but this straight-out refusal has me stumped.

'What?' I stammer.

Tom slips his bag off his shoulder and props it up against the wall. 'No,' he says again. 'That's not how it goes.' He reaches for my hands, which hang lifeless by my sides, numb with the dread of what I've just done, closes his fingers around my wrists and draws me down to the floor. I try to resist, stay standing up, but his pull is too strong – not violent, but forceful – and we both end up sitting, loosely cross-legged, in the hallway. He keeps a tight grip on my hands; they have gone icy cold.

'Talk to me,' he says.

'Talk to you,' I repeat, low as a growl, and suddenly all my fears, all my doubts, all the questions I've asked and couldn't answer, the terrible scenarios I've had to live through that brought me here turn into indignation. 'Talk to you? You haven't talked to me in weeks!'

I try to jerk my hands away, but he won't let me. He gives a tiny nod, an admission, without breaking the contact of our eyes.

'Nevertheless,' he says. 'Talk to me.'

I take a deep inhale and breathe it out: 'You had a girl's phone number.'

A strange thing happens to his face: a flash of confusion, and then a softening, a slackness and what – unexpectedly, illogically – looks like relief. I can't work out what it's doing there. It's fleeting; the next moment, his jaw hardens.

'That's it?' he says, in a coarse, gritty whisper. 'That's what you were about to leave me for?' I've never seen his eyes so narrow; I don't like the way he glares at me. 'You weren't even gonna ask me? For fuck's sake, Anna, you weren't even gonna give me a chance?'

I start in shock. Tom never swears at me, but it's not that, and it isn't his anger: it's how disappointed he sounds that flips the world upside down. From where I stood, before, I was the one who was hurt.

'It was written in eyeliner,' I say pathetically, and I'm almost glad when he doesn't respond. But I wish he wouldn't look at me that way.

'Ask me,' he says, and it's like a heavy stone dropped from a great height, hitting the ground with a deep, dreadful thud that resonates through me and makes my hair stand on end. I drop my eyes away from the challenge of his gaze. My arms ache from holding them out all this time.

'Why did you have that girl's number?'

'She gave it to me. At that work do, the launch party. She was somebody's friend. She gave it to me and I said I wouldn't call her. I didn't call her. I have no intention of calling her.' He stops short, breathless, though he hasn't raised his voice.

I make a small whimpering sound in the back of my throat; it comes out of me involuntarily, and I gulp to swallow it down. My chest heaves.

'Look at me, Anna,' he says, and I do. 'I had no intention of calling her. Anyone. I would never... Don't you know that?' The hardness is gone and it's my undoing, and I shudder with the tears I'm fighting to hold back. I don't know how I feel.

Tom uncrosses his legs and shuffles over to wrap them around me. He lets go of my hands and leans in to gather me in his arms. I stiffen for a moment, and give in, and press my forehead onto his, our noses squashed together. Our lips brush against each other as we speak.

'You should know.'

'I know. I'm sorry.'

'I'm sorry too. About the not talking. I've been preoccupied. I didn't realise how it looked.'

'I should have told you.'

'I should have thought about it.'

'I'm an idiot.'

'We're both idiots.'

Stupid, grateful, relieved: that's how I feel. Ashamed. Still reeling from the shock of what I almost did. But calm. Somewhere inside me, calm. It isn't over, but we'll forgive each other. There was a bump in the road and I tripped over it and hurt my knee, and then I tried to run and hide like an injured animal. But Tom knew not to let me. I don't know how he knew, but I'm grateful. Stupid. Relieved. Embarrassed that I let a scrape frighten me so much. A little wiser. Maybe I'll know, next time, when the road is uneven. Maybe I'll take Tom's hand so neither of us falls.

We whisper some words – love, trust, sorry – and kiss, and peel our faces away, both of them clammy with my tears. We help each other to our feet, a bit wobbly from being still for so long.

'The front doors needs oiling,' I tell him.

It's not a problem, but it's our door and we need to fix it. We can fix it, together, so it doesn't creak anymore.

No: it isn't over. That's not how it goes.

***

40 years, and Tom is being stoical.

'How does it feel, to be middle-aged?' I tease. 'Are you freaking out?'

'No,' he says, but I think he's freaking out a little, so we're having a quiet evening at home, keeping to ourselves. Tomorrow, a Sunday, we have agreed to spend the day at Chris and Sylvia's, an unofficial gathering that will inevitably turn into a party, and Tom will submit, good-naturedly, to the wishes and songs and celebrations, and sticky little girl hands in his hair as he dances with his goddaughter in his arms. Tomorrow we will be grateful for all that, for our friends, and be friendly; we will be social and smile and make jokes and laugh at other people's jokes, but tonight we don't want anybody else.

We both cook. Tom makes his signature pasta dish, tried once and longed for ever since in an obscure little restaurant in Rome: linguini with a thick sauce of fresh tomatoes, melted scamorza cheese and a hint of chilli, with basil leaves torn off our plant scattered on top. I wasn't with him on that trip to Rome – it was before I met him – but Tom claims his version is nearly as good as the original, and promises, every time we have it, to take me there one day. I make rosemary garlic bread from scratch, using a pizza dough recipe, and a rocket and spinach salad with crushed walnuts and a honey and balsamic dressing. We have Mars bars for dessert; neither of us remembers who started it – one of us must have brought one home – but we've been obsessed with those things for weeks. I have also bought a bottle of wine, which I rarely do, and spent a whole ten pounds on it, which makes feel equally proud and appalled. I'm playing at being a grown up, with Tom turning forty and a bottle of wine as my props. We have no wine glasses but we have a set of those short, stubby ones – I think they're for whisky – so we use those, but only fill them halfway up. I raise mine and wish him happy birthday and Tom frowns – every time, the same story, all these years.

We sit on the sofa after dinner and I reach behind me, between the cushions, and pull out a small rectangle wrapped in newspaper. I hand it to Tom.

'It's not a present,' I tell him, but it's gift-wrapped and it's the best that I can give him, of myself. It's a story I've written about our story so far, and I've had it printed and bound into a book. I hand it over but I don't explain it, and the title printed on the cover is "Untitled", because you can't define a story that hasn't ended and you can't give a name to an unfinished thing. I'm giving him the best that I can give him, a work in progress, and when he reads it he will know what it's about.

When he reads it he'll know that I've noticed the bumps in the road, that I saw them and sidestepped them, but not always. That there were times when I've tripped and fallen, and scraped my knees; that I've come across trees blown into the path, ripped from the ground and lying on their sides, all gnarly roots and pointed branches, avalanches and floods and long stretches of road where there was nothing much to look at, no twists and no surprises. That there were times when I considered turning off, taking another road, tempted by the patch of green that I could make out in the distance. That I considered it but didn't do it, because I learnt, with time, that I wasn't walking this road alone. I learnt how to reach for his hand when I fell, and let him help me up; I learnt to let him see the bruises and the cuts, even if he couldn't fix them. I learnt that we could get each other over the obstacles, or around them, and that if one of us couldn't see the way, the other might. I learnt that there would always be more twists in the road, and to be grateful for the quiet times, the uneventful strolls, just holding someone's hand and walking. I learnt that every patch of green will wilt and dry if you don't look after it and even then, even with your best efforts, tending to it on your hands and knees, a frost might come along, or a long draught, and kill it, and you'll have to start again, with only handfuls of soil and a single, tiny seed. A magic seed, if you believe in it, like the bean that took Jack up into the sky.

Tom unwraps the book and holds it up, almost reverentially, between the pads of his hands, thumbs out, fingers straight, leaving the whole of the cover in view. There isn't much to it: a glossy white background, *Untitled*, and my name. He opens it up on the first page, the dedication: "For Tom, for his birthday, for every day."

'Can I read it now?' he asks, eyes bright and eager, like a child.

I nod, brush his cheek with the back of my hand, and stand up.

'I'll leave you to it,' I say.

He reads it, hunched over on the sofa, elbows close to his body, shoulders curled up over bent knees, his face practically buried inside the book. He reads it without a break, without a word, only the flutter of pages turning and the low grumble of traffic on the high road behind the flat. He reads it as I wait, nervous for his reaction, excited, impatient and clueless, because I cannot see his face. I go into the kitchen so I don't hover over him, wash up the dishes from dinner, tidy up, and make a cup of tea that I don't want. I find my glass of wine and drink that, instead. I smoke a cigarette. I wait.

When I return to the living room, Tom is sitting up with the book balanced on his knees, and both hands over it, holding it in place. His head is lowered and his eyes are closed. He hears me come in and stirs, places the book on the sofa beside him and pats it, once, as if to reassure himself it's there, or the book that he hasn't forgotten it. But he still doesn't lift his head until I take the last few steps and stand in front of him. And then he looks up, slowly, and there's something watery about his eyes, but determined, and he doesn't say anything, he just holds out his hand. I take it, and he draws me in and I kneel down between his legs and wrap my arms around his waist and rest my cheek on his thigh. And Tom folds over again, curls himself over me, and we become what we've always been: one strange, rounded thing, the magic seed that will keep growing gardens every time we plant it.

Twelve

A man ran down a South London high street in the rain, holding the hood of his top stretched over his head with both hands, like a canopy. He was running because he'd been caught out by the rain, the rain he didn't see coming, but also because he was impatient. He might have run even without the rain; even on a clear, sunny day he'd have wanted to run towards this. He ran, threading his way expertly through the thick pedestrian traffic that crowded these South London pavements, twisting and contorting his body like a dancer to fit into the gaps between people and pushchairs and shopping trolleys stuffed full of vegetables from the market and clandestine bicycles, and get there faster.

He came to a stop outside a bookstore, pulled his hood back, tugged at his hair, and stepped through the door. At the counter, he waited patiently for the assistant to look up.

'Good morning,' he said. 'I'm looking for a book.' He paused, laughed at himself and gave the girl a self-conscious smile. 'Obviously,' he added. 'This being a bookstore and everything.' He told her the title. 'It's new. It's just come out.'

The assistant giggled at his embarrassment and rattled away on her keyboard, without taking her eyes off his face.

'Yes,' she said, and tapped the screen – click, click, click – with a purple fingernail. 'Right there, on the new releases table.' She used the same fingernail to point.

The man thanked her and stepped aside so that the next customer could take his place, but he made no further move for some time. He had run here, down the high street, through the crowds like a person possessed, but now he hesitated. This was a significant moment and he'd imagined it many times, but he hadn't imagined it like this. Its weight, when borne alone, was heavy and tinged with sadness, the pride, the words he'd say, the smiles he'd give made redundant by her absence. Is it possible to celebrate someone who isn't there? He would have to try. He would bear it alone, with pride.

He approached the display cautiously, aware of what a strange sight he must make, a man afraid of a book, and stopped again when he saw it, multiple copies stacked high and neatly on the tabletop. He stopped to take it in, this first sight of it; to put some ceremony into this occasion that would otherwise be just a man buying a book on a South London high street.

He made it to the table and picked up the top copy. He ran his fingers over the cover and down the spine, turned it around and around in his hands.

'Well done, baby,' he whispered, 'I knew you'd do it,' as he'd imagined he would. But he hadn't imagined it this way, the words spoken under his breath in a near-empty bookstore on a rainy morning, his hand holding nothing but the book. He'd never have imagined it like this.

He opened the book up on the dedications page and read the unusual message that was there: *You know who you are.*

His head spun. He staggered back to the counter

'You found it, then,' said the girl brightly, but he was distracted and only slid the book across, along with his card. He felt bad afterwards, for not returning her smile.

He took the book home, back through the high street and the back streets in the rain, and started to read. It was a short book and he finished it the next morning, having read for most of the day and almost through the night, with a few hours of restless, dreamless sleep in between. He flicked back to the beginning – *You know who you are* – and, still in bed, reached for his phone. He checked the time, 10:35, scrolled through his contacts and placed a call to a disconnected number. He stared at the screen, tried again, holding the phone out in front of him and squinting at it with mistrust: the same curt message, the same ominous tone.

He sat up in his bed, propped up against the pillow, and made another call.

'Hello mate,' he said when it was answered. 'I didn't wake you? Good. Listen, is your girl around? Yes please, let me speak to her.'

He waited for the phone to be passed on, for the surprised voice on the other end. He said good morning, how are you, and then he asked his question.

Listened to the answer.

'Oh!,' he said presently. 'No, I didn't know. No, not for a while. Yes, please. Hang on.' He groped on the bedside table for a pen and something to write on: a used rail ticket. 'OK. Hit me.'

He took down a number.

'Thank you,' he said. 'I'll see you both soon,' and hung up.

He didn't call straight away. He sat in his bed for a while, with the book on his lap and the phone in his hand. You know who you are, he thought.

And then Jack dialled the number and called Anna.

*

It was a long time ago, now, that this happened: I stood behind the door of our flat and when Jack came in I killed his halfway smile with my words and told him it was over. He didn't say no. He didn't ask why. He slipped back into the evening and closed the door gently behind him, as if he'd never been there at all. I didn't stop him. I didn't stop myself. I didn't run after him, and he just let me go. We made mistakes; we were mistaken. We didn't think. We didn't know. And time passed.

Time passed, elsewhere, with other people, in other lives. Elsewhere, and Jack slipped away like he had never been at all, but he had been and so had I. We had been things to each other, once. And there are certain things that time cannot touch.

Time passed, and made changes. There were years and birthdays and celebrations spent elsewhere, with other people. There were reasons. There were questions that were never asked, answers that were never asked for, answers that could not be given, or received. There were stories, filling the spaces between what happened and what could have been, between the done and the should have done; fiction building a bridge of words between fact and fate. There were what ifs that grew into alternative lives, spelling out the difference between ends and endings. There were dreams of a commonplace reality that had been pushed off the map of this world. And the world carried on, regardless, rushing forward in the relentless slipstream of time. And there were things that changed. And there were things that stayed the same, untouchable, untouched.

There is a Neverland, a place in time, a land that fell through the cracks between then and not yet, but it can yet be found. There is another kind of time that does this. A time that takes you back to where you belong.

***

This is not one of my dreams. This is not one of my stories. Jack calls me on my new number, a number he's never called before. It's been six months since I saw him, since I watched him cross over to a place I had no permission to enter, past barriers that I couldn't breach. I take a breath and press the phone to my ear.

'I'm so glad you called,' I blurt out, without meaning to, but no one has ever accused me of being cool.

'Oh,' he says, taken aback, 'right. Hi!' and I can hear the lift of pleasure in his voice, unexpectedly there despite my fears. Mine is tentative, cautious, a toe dipped in the sea on the cusp of seasons changing, to check if it'll welcome me in or stop my blood solid with its frozen embrace.

'Hello Jack.'

'You're back,' he informs me.

'I'm back,' I agree.

'To stay?'

I nod in vigorous affirmation, though he can't see me. 'I'm not going anywhere.'

'Good. Coffee?'

'Sorry?'

'I mean – can we meet up?

'What, now?' My brain trips on the implications, and throws up practicalities: I have to be at work in an hour. My sensible brain, conspicuous in its dayglo vest even through the haze, holding up a stop sign.

'Now, later, tomorrow, the day after. Whenever.' And then he says something that makes my heart, the heart he holds, thump and crash against my chest. He says: 'I think it's time.'

I'd forgotten about this: the breathlessness, the heightened heartbeat, the blood riding your veins like a rollercoaster, bringing the idle places screaming back to life. Sensations that have lain dormant, on standby, blinking a pinprick of light. A heart that has only fluttered to a steady, regular beat. I've missed it, this exhilarating terror, this terrifying hope. It's been good, to live my life on an even keel, untroubled by desires; not hopeless, but hoping for nothing that I couldn't touch. It's been good but I've done it, and here it is, now: time.

I don't comment. I don't ask if he means the time that passes, or the other kind of time. 'Tonight,' I say. 'I can meet you tonight.'

The sea is tepid where I'm standing, in the surf, gentle waves lapping over my feet and the foam tickling my ankles. But these are shallow waters and they tell me nothing about the deep. You never know, with the ocean, what it might do when you drift further and further from the safety of the coast. What pockets of cold it might be hosting in its belly, what vicious currents it might send to pull you under and swallow you whole. What monsters, what mermaids, what sunken worlds, what sunken ships. You'll never know unless you trust in this thing that cannot be trusted, and dive in with your eyes open. Or can you stay on the beach and imagine what it would feel like to be swimming, and build castles in the sand and turn your head before you can see the ocean rising up and washing them away.

I'm cautious on the cusp of maybe, and maybe it's now. Maybe the time is now. Maybe that's what he means.

We don't know how to be when we meet. We don't know what to do with our hands. I stand rigid as a statue, my arms stiff by my sides, while Jack grasps for my shoulder and jerks away immediately, the moment his fingers connect, as if he's been burnt. He settles for my wrist, and we end up locked in an awkward clinch, somewhere between arm wrestling and a handshake. Bewildered, we both tilt our heads curiously at this twist we've gotten ourselves into, unclasp our hands and laugh.

'Hug?' he suggests, throwing his arms open.

'Good plan,' I say as I step into them, but now it's body against body and we're confused again, and we're patting each other on the back, patting down those unsettling feelings that kick up against the surface, disturbed from their slumber and demanding recognition.

We pull apart and even our smiles don't know how to behave and they twinkle, unresolved, on our faces, flickering from reserved to manic to hopeful and still not finding their place.

'Well,' Jack says. 'Wow.' And I suppose these words will do as much as any others.

We go into the café, a generic café that could be anywhere, that could have tumbled out my dreams and landed on any London street, except this one happens to be in Camden and I am wide awake. We order our coffees at the counter and burrow in a corner, on a sofa that sags in the middle and sends us sliding into each other as soon as we sit down. Nervous giggles, and we make subtle adjustments, but we're connected shoulder to hip.

'Welcome back to town,' Jack says as a girl in an old-fashioned lace apron bends over the table to deliver our coffees. He lifts his cup and knocks it into mine and a splash of coffee sloshes over the rim. He swabs it with his finger as it trickles down the side, and licks it off, and he means nothing by this gesture, but I am entranced, and I'm embarrassed; I am holding my breath. The waitress catches my eye and smiles and I realise she's been watching, watching me watching Jack, and I give her a shrug.

Jack stirs sugar into his coffee and plays with his spoon. We glance at each other, faces still undecided on expressions, and sink back into the sofa with matching sighs – both exaggerated, because neither of us is entirely relaxed. My pulse has been racing since this morning, and Jack is restless, like I've never seen him before.

'So. How have you been?'

And I tell him the truth, that I've been well. Better. Happy. Drawing circles in the sky, maybe, but not drifting. I know where I am. I tell him the truth as it occurs to me because, for all my gratitude, I hadn't realised, until now, until I hear myself describing it to Jack, exactly what it is that I am grateful for.

'I feel good in myself,' I tell him, and my smile is genuine, not brave.

But this is not a catching-up session, and it's not about coffee, and now Jack leans forward and places his cup onto the saucer and his hand on my knee. Our eyes flit down and up again, to meet in the space between us.

'About Athens,' he begins. 'I think I got it wrong.'

'What happened?' I ask, at long last.

'Your flat, and Robert living there. I thought that you were still–'.

I shake my head frantically and interrupt him. 'No. We weren't.'

Jack swallows, hard. 'Why was he there?'

I try to think of a way to put this that makes sense. It isn't complicated, after all. 'Because he was an arsehole.'

Jack cracks up: amusement and, I think, relief. Relief is definitely what I feel, that I can finally tell him – shout it – how bad it was.

'He just wouldn't move out! It was a fucking nightmare! Oh my god, Jack, you have no idea! It's a miracle I didn't kill the little fucker.' Jack laughs again and there's no guilt. If I owed Robert anything, I've paid him back in full.

But Jack turns serious again, sombre even. 'I'm sorry,' he says. 'I panicked. I should have asked you, but I assumed. I almost left when you told me, you know. I almost went to the airport, there and then.'

'It might have been better if you had. I might have known something was up. I could have explained.' The thought of that is hard to deal with, even from this distance; it sends me spinning into a whole new vortex of what ifs. I think Jack is in there with me, because he sighs deeply and looks at me with eyes hinting regret.

'Regardless,' he says eventually. 'I'm glad I didn't. I couldn't. But the next morning I just couldn't stay. It was fight or flight,' he adds, and snorts bitterly at this inadvertent, perfectly inappropriate joke. I am not in the mood for laughing.

'I wish you'd fought.' But the gravity of my own tone unsettles me, and I relent. 'I actually had fantasies of you beating the shit out of Robert,' I confide, finding an edge of humour to grab hold of.

'I think I might have enjoyed that,' he grins. 'Hey. Are you crying?'

I didn't cry when he left. Not as I watched him go, not as I stood in the vacuum of his departure and relived it, not sitting down on a cold, hard airport bench, not on the train back into town. I didn't cry when I got home, or after. I am, apparently, crying now. I don't know when it started, but my face is damp.

'It's alright,' Jack soothes, as he raises his hand to cup my chin, running his thumb down my cheek, and the simple tenderness of this gesture overthrows me. 'Baby. It's alright.'

'Please,' I whisper helplessly. 'Don't call me that.'

'But – OK. OK.' He takes his hand away and sits up straighter, and it's the same hand that had been on my knee, so now he's not touching me and, despite what I just said, I feel bereft. Which makes Jack's question – a question he's asked me before – chillingly pertinent. His voice rings a little metallic.

'Anna. What do you want?'

He didn't let me answer last time, but now he's waiting. He waits and I think, and it's like I'm in a room full of walls, more walls than a room should have, and they're all covered floor to ceiling with letters, blocks of letters like those word search puzzles, where you scan each line for the words to solve the riddle. I know the words I need are in here somewhere, the words he's waiting for, but they elude me. I search the vertical, the horizontal, the diagonal; I squint and look sideways and turn myself upside down, but I cannot make them out. I can't solve the riddle that will release me from this room. There are too many words, too many walls.

I turn to look at Jack, return to him empty-handed, begging for mercy. Pleading with him to let me out. There's a dip of his head, a concession.

'OK,' he says softly. 'Never mind.' But he doesn't let the silence settle. He breathes and broadens his shoulders, and hands me something that looks like a key.

'But is there anything you want to ask me?'

And here it is, a thing that rarely happens. A chance to get closure, to grab that door he closed so gently all those years ago and slam it shut. To know for certain. The phone number, Jayne, his silence. The distance I was afraid to cross. And whether I would have found him, if I'd dared, on the other side. The why did you and the why didn't you and the what now. The years in between, the years of wondering, of following the tangled up threads of an incomplete, heartbroken logic: unravelled. Laid out as facts. But when was anything worth knowing based on facts?

I have suspected that the planet I've been orbiting was Jack, but Jack is not the sun. He's just another ship, like me, launched from the same place but on a mission of his own. It's only answers I've been circling, answers to the questions that sent me into orbit in the first place, but the questions are redundant and the answers obsolete: they do not have the power to release me or bring me back. But we have met, Jack and I, on our separate journeys. Our paths have crossed again – a chance encounter or a predetermined course, coordinates set ahead of time – and the only question, now, must be whether we're both ready to land in the same place, or whether we'll drift past each other and continue on to somewhere else.

It's a Pandora's box this key will open. It is a test, though Jack doesn't mean it that way; he's only trying to give me a gift. I twist it between my fingers, but I am no longer tempted. I hand it back, and I can only hope he understands: none of it matters. There is nothing that I need to know.

'No,' I say, 'actually. There isn't.' And then, reciprocal, if we are doing this, 'And you? Is there anything you want to ask?'

Jack holds my gaze, steady, for a long time, and it's my turn to wait.

'Yes,' he says eventually. 'Which one?'

'I'm sorry? Which one what?'

He doesn't smile. His face doesn't change, but there is a veiled presence, a reference to an enigmatic smile in the way he moves. He reaches into his bag and pulls out a book, my book. He puts it down on the table, between our half-empty coffee cups. He puts it down gently but it's as if he's slammed it down for the impact it makes. He keeps his hand on it for a moment, then slides it away and sits back. And he asks me again.

'Which one?'

Alternative endings. The one where I wait behind the door, wielding the words that will kill Jack's smile, but he disarms me. The one where I almost do it, but change my mind and just smile back at him as he comes through the door. The one where he leaves and I run after him, barefoot down the street; where I catch up to him on the Broadway, by a bus stop at rush hour in the September drizzle, and burst into tears, with an audience of twenty damp Londoners, and cut my foot on a piece of glass and let Jack carry me home. The one where he'd never stray and Jayne is just a girl whom he doesn't call. The one where he does, but he finds his way back and we move on together, hand in hand down our bumpy, happy road. The one where a piece of paper is a piece of paper and I put it in the bin, where it belongs. The one where I don't let the silence intimidate me, but stand up to it and observe it, pay it my respects, and let it go.

And this one: the end, and all the years in between. The one I would never have chosen. But given the choice, given the chance, given everything that's happened, the damage we caused, the mistakes we made, for all the happy endings that I wrote to replace it, this is the one that brought us here.

This is not one of my stories. Jack and I in a café, sitting together, side by side. I break the silence.

'This,' I say. 'This one.' And this time I watch him smile all the way through, because I've finally said the right thing. No matter where it takes us from here, I've finally got it right.

It might be minutes later, or hours, that the waitress nudges us back with a cough.

'I'm so sorry,' she says, 'but we're closing. Actually, we've been closed for a while. I didn't want to disturb you, but I have to go now.'

What have we been doing that would warrant this kindness? She's locked the door and turned the lights down, she's cleaned around us as we sat in stillness, holding hands; she's straightened the chairs and tables, filled up the sugar pots and blown the candles out. What did she see that made her do this? What did we look like, through her eyes?

Jack and I spring up, embarrassed, muttering mantras of thank yous and sorrys, and try to tip her, but she just smiles and shakes her head and says 'No worries' and, as she unlocks the door to let us out, 'Good luck'.

Out on the pavement, where a cold wind swirls litter around our feet, we smile inanely for a moment, and then I say I'd better go.

'Better?' Jack says. 'No.'

'What?'

'You're not going.'

'I'm not?'

'No. I'm taking you home.'

'Home where?' As if it matters where he takes me.

'Camberwell?' An apologetic mumble.

'Camberwell.' I wince. As if I give a fuck. 'But I suppose it is the nicer part?'

And we laugh all the way to the station because we both know such a place does not exist. Maybe that's our Neverland then, sprinkled with dust blown up from the street: the nicer part of Camberwell. That's where it is. And that's where we're going, no longer making circles. I have landed. I have been called back home.

Jack and I in bed, naked, looking up at the ceiling. In Camberwell, in Neverland, wherever. Underneath the duvet, our fingers are entwined. We could have fallen straight out of my dreams, but we are only drowsy, not asleep. I turn on my side to face him, and he does the same. We adjust our pillows and bring our noses to touch.

'This,' I say again, the same answer to another question, now that the riddle has been solved. 'This is what I want.'

Jack gasps. 'My body? That's all you want me for?'

'Yes,' I say. 'And for everything.' For this man, and the talking and the silences, the birthdays we missed and the celebrations that we'll have, the years spent elsewhere, with other people, the people we were and the people we've become, the cuts and the bruises, patches of green and wilted grass and magic seeds, and the bumpy, happy road ahead, no matter where it leads. And in the space between us, the thing that time couldn't touch.

'Everything,' Jack repeats. 'I think I can live with that.'

This is not one of my stories. This is the story of Jack and me. We're not done yet.

***

(Not) the end

Gratitude

To my early readers, Susanne, Peter, Ariadne, Dennis and Margarita: thank you for your support, your feedback, and your enthusiasm. Sorry I made you cry sometimes.

To Eileen, who always supports me.

To everyone who said they wanted to read my next book: here it is.

To Marshall: I'm not saying I couldn't have done this without you, but it would have been a lot less fun. This applies to most things I do. Thank you.

About the author

Daphne Kapsali was born in Athens in 1978, but that was a bit of a mistake on the part of the universe, because she's actually a Londoner. She lived in that wonderful, terrible city very happily on and off since 1996, doing a variety of fun and badly-paid jobs, until she realised she was a writer, whereupon she promptly made herself homeless and unemployed to spend a few months living alone on a small Greek island and writing full-time. She dubbed this project *100 days of solitude* and the result, one hundred stories brought together under the same title, is now available in paperback and on Kindle. *you can't name an unfinished thing*, also produced during her stint as a reclusive author, is her first published novel. Both will be bestsellers.

When she's done being a recluse on remote islands, Daphne will be moving back to London, where she plans to carry on writing and take over the world with her crazy genius boyfriend.

***

If you have enjoyed this book, please take a moment to rate it, or write a review on Amazon. Thank you!

Get in touch:

www.daphnekapsali.com

www.facebook.com/reclusiveauthor

Printed in Great Britain
by Amazon